TO Flyss +
+ FRank

inspire me

MW01170095

CONSCIENCE
POINT

A PILGRIM'S LANDING MYSTERY

ROZ SIEGEL

X

Roz

ARBITRARY PRESS

For Randy and Maren, and Janine and Larry. And for my grandchildren, Hallie, Evan, Willa, Josh and Eli.

A special thanks to Peter Alson, who fearlessly edited many wild patches, asked the right questions and, with intelligence, patience and insight, made sure all the words were in their proper place. And thanks also to Maeve Norton for her fabulous cover design.

Chapter One

Oh, Ahab! What shall be grand in thee, it must needs be plucked
at from the skies, and dived for in the deep, and featured in the
unbodied air!

—**Herman Melville**, *Moby Dick*

"You're searching for a word that means when two people live together
and aren't married. Seems to me 'Cohabitation' is the word you're
looking for."

There was a dissatisfied grunt from the other end of the telephone line.

I stared up at the white marble ceiling of the library, but couldn't think of
anything further to add.

Besides, it was already a little after 5 pm, and I was tired of answering questions and stamping library cards in this gorgeous new library that somehow had
not adopted electronic check-out.

"Let me connect you with Research," I said.

I let the phone ring four or five times for show. I knew there would be no
answer. Winston Worthington Fowl, head of the Research Department and a
three-named descendant of the Pilgrims (who made up a sizable percentage of
the residents of the aptly named Pilgrim's Landing), rarely answered his phone

after two o'clock. He was either asleep from one too many nips out of his silver flask or he'd gone home.

I figured the caller would get bored and hang up.

No such luck.

"How about lovers?" I offered the caller. "Or roommates?"

The caller had in mind something "sinful."

Did this amount to phone sex in Pilgrim's Landing?

"Sorry," I said. "Sinful thoughts were not included in my Library Science Program. Try a clergyman."

My caller said, "Thank you," and hung up.

Such good manners the locals had! It made me feel a little ashamed of my snarky response. The caller was probably just a lonely old guy reaching out for some human contact, not a pervert seeking a thrill.

I'd been finding it hard to ditch my New York City attitude—one downside of having recently moved from the city where I'd lived for the past 45 years to the small eastern Long Island haven of Pilgrim's Landing.

I suppose if your family had lived in a place since 1640, settled by a bunch of fanatics who pushed the practice of honesty, purity, and correct behavior, there were some cultural traits, such as good manners, that were bred into you. Traits I obviously had neither inherited nor learned. I was still experiencing culture shock. Cement instead of water, sea everywhere. Even though the cabin I'd rented was located on a small hill, seagulls filled the sky and settled on my roof. Puddles of water appeared in my front yard and then magically disappeared. Crispy crackers on my kitchen table turned soggy after one day.

Wherever I was, I could hear the pounding of the surf—the heartbeat of the town.

It was quieter than New York City but not the quiet I had expected. The 6 a.m. train tooted each morning; twice a day the volunteer fire department's emergency sirens blared.

The church bells rang every hour, and the racoons rattled my garbage cans all night. The mournful blasts of the foghorn sounded during the night; a chorus of birds awakened me at dawn.

Woodpeckers tapped most of the day outside my bedroom window, and a sparrow made a nest on top of the light on my porch, complaining loudly each time I entered or left my cabin.

What struck me most, however, was the regularity of the sounds that surrounded me. I waited for the train whistle as if I were going on a trip; I waited for the emergency siren each evening to signal a time for my vodka martini. Even the birds and animals were regular in their routines, and regularity was what had governed Pilgrims Landing since 1640.

My good friend Ellen Hinkley, a Pilgrim's Landing native and my guide to this new world, had left the library a little early to meet up with her fiancé Eddie, the library's IT guy. Even though Ellen was a few years younger than me and was the kind of woman who kept a sewing kit in her purse while I carried a pair of stiletto shoes (which could be used as weapons or adornments depending upon the occasion), we had formed a lasting bond.

She was quite cute when she let her hair down and put on her bright red lipstick (although she would have looked a lot better if she ditched no-iron shirts two sizes too large in favor of a sweater—a suggestion I didn't make for fear of embarrassing her).

"Remember to take your slicker when you're ready to go home. There's a storm coming," Ellen had warned on her way out.

"Computer says all clear this evening."

"Nope. Storms a'comin. I can smell it and hear the splash of the waves on the beach. You grow up here, the rhythms of the sea begin to infiltrate your blood stream. Founded by the pilgrims but ruled by Neptune."

I glanced out the windows overlooking the bay. The sky was such a clear, deep purple, it almost took my breath away. Not a rain cloud in sight.

I locked the door and turned off the lights in the main reading room. I was in no hurry to go home to my lonely little bungalow in the woods.

The main floor of the library, where I worked, was polished marble, white with a thin threading of green, as if the grass outside had found its way in. The air smelled of the cucumbers and carrots from the farm stand across the street, and when the lights were out, I could see the stars in the sky through the large plate-glass windows.

I had grown up frequenting dark, musty little branch libraries in Brooklyn, with their sagging shelves and coffee-stained books. The Pilgrim's Landing library, by contrast, with its facade of columns, reminiscent of a Greek temple, and huge and welcoming glass windows, was a perfect monument to learning.

The long reading tables were golden oak, the chandeliers hand-blown glass, the shelves tall and straight the way the pilgrims must have been. And books were only the beginning. There were shelves of movies to be borrowed, tapes and CDs, large-print and audio books. There was a whole room of computers, printers, a copy and scanning machine, and a children's section filled with light.

Most people in town never locked their doors. The intimacy of the townsfolk seemed to me a guarantee of honesty. The guy who ran the tackle shop would never show up with a watch belonging to the veterinarian. The beautician would never wear a gold necklace that everyone in town knew had been a fifth anniversary present from the yoga teacher's husband. Ellen told me I didn't even have to lock the library after leaving at night. But I did anyway. New York habits were hard to shake.

As I wandered around, turning off lights, I ended up in the children's section, which, though I tried not to let it, caused a pang. I had failed to produce a child of my own—or rather, the one I had produced was stillborn—so I had a special place in my heart (as well as an ache) for other people's children. There was no shortage of them in this town. And clearly, they were valued, as was reflected in the design of this section of the library. Here was a whole world of wonder and cheer. The scaled down oak tables and chairs smelled of fresh wood and polish. On each small table, there was a stack of books.

Here was Curious George, clinging to the man with the yellow hat.

Here was Winnie the Pooh and Christopher Robin.

Here was Babar and Celeste.

I picked up *Alice in Wonderland* and wedged myself into one of the small children's chairs. Just as I was settling in, there was a loud banging on the outside door.

At almost the same moment came a booming clap of thunder and a flash of lightning.

My watch told me it was 5:30. The library was officially closed.

The knocking on the door intensified. So did the thunder.

It was hard to imagine any kind of emergency that required a librarian after closing time.

But when I tried to stand up, I could not extricate my rear end from the chair and ended up crab-walking to the door still attached to it.

As I unlocked and pulled back the heavy wood door, a gust of sea spray hit my face, and then, along with another terrifying clap of thunder, a bolt of lightning silhouetted a tall figure against the briefly illuminated sky, his dark hair pulled back in some kind of knot. It was as if Neptune himself had decided to pay a visit to the Pilgrim's Landing library.

Nevertheless, a rule was a rule.

"We're closed," I said, trying to ignore the white T-shirt stretched tight across his muscular chest and the electric blue-green eyes that were the color of the bay. It was hard sounding authoritative with my butt still firmly locked into a child's chair.

He glanced at his watch. "Says here it's only 4:50."

I shook my head. "Sorry."

"You couldn't make an exception?" He waved a book in front of me, the title of which I couldn't see.

What I *could* see was a man who could motivate a public servant to break the rules.

"Besides," he said. "It looks like you need my help." Without asking me or saying anything more, this handsome stranger put one very strong arm around the seatback of my new appendage and, with a quick twist, dislodged my body from the chair and into his arms.

He had a fresh, slightly salty smell, like laundry dried by the sea.

Freed, I turned on the lights.

"Thanks." I started to explain how it had happened, but he held up a hand.

"Could happen to anyone. My apologies for the intrusion. It's all because of this book!" He waved it in front of me again, and this time I saw what it was.

"*Moby Dick*! You're reading *Moby Dick*!"

"Yes, that's why I'm here. The last chapter is missing! Someone tore it out! Can you believe that? I saw the movie when I was a kid—but I forget the ending."

I was tempted to say that everyone dies except Ismael and the fish, but now that he was on my line, I was in no hurry to cut him loose.

"We should have another copy, but let me guess, your forefathers came over on the Santa Maria with Christopher Columbus and you're interested in reviving the whaling industry."

"There was a boat all right, but it was a freighter out of Palermo around 1920 and I've been fishing these waters myself ever since I was a kid. Gian-Carlo Messini. My friends call me Messi."

His long fingers wrapped around my own.

"I'll get you another copy."

I went off to get the book.

"We have a book club," I said when I came back, handing him the replacement copy. "Meets every Friday night. "

"Are they reading *Moby Dick*?"

"*Pride and Prejudice*. Jane Austen."

"I think I'll skip that one. Thanks for letting me in. "

I walked him to the door.

There was another clap of thunder, and suddenly the rain came down in sheets.

"Wait! You'll get drenched. I'm sure it will stop soon!"

Messi shook his head. "This is an all-nighter. But don't worry about me. I walk between the raindrops."

He paused for a minute. "What did you say your name was?"

"Sandra Nussbaum. My friends call me Sandy."

He bent over me, his face so close I could see a small scar on his upper lip.

"I suggest in the future you be more careful where you put your pretty little ass, Sandy Nussbaum. Lots of sharks in these waters." And with that, he disappeared into the night.

***

"Oh Messi!" Ellen said, looking up from the pile of books she was stamping. "So, you met Messi. What'd you think of him?"

I shrugged. "I dunno. Handsome guy. Has a watch that runs slow. Prefers to borrow books instead of buying them. *Not* descended from the pilgrims."

Ellen laughed. "Certainly not. Actually, he hangs out in Sands End most of the time. Full-time commercial fisherman. Grew up there. Not married—at least if he is, he keeps it a secret. Had a girl a while back from Pilgrim's Landing. Marna Van Dugan. She was one of those pilgrim people you talk about. Dutch heritage. They lived together for a while. That's probably when he got the library card. But she drowned. A couple of years ago. Got quite a write-up in all the local papers. Messi took it hard. At least that's what I heard. He disappeared for a while. Thought maybe he was gone for good. I wonder why he's showing up now?"

A gorgeous man with a tragedy in his background! More *Wuthering Heights* than *Pride and Prejudice*! Messi was becoming more interesting by the second.

Too bad the library was open till 9 p.m. on Thursdays. I'd have to wait until after closing check out the old newspaper reports of what happened to his pilgrim girlfriend.

The good news was that Messi was unmarried. The bad news was that he was a fisherman. Not that I had anything against fishermen. As a group I prefer them to cops. The problem? I don't like fish.

Well—I would cross that bridge when I came to it. For the moment, I wanted to find out whatever I could about this Marna Van Dugan and the whole drowning situation.

As soon as the library clock hit nine, I went over to our newspaper archives and tried to look up the local stories. We only kept one year of the local papers on file. After that you could access the website of the newspaper from the library computer. I went downstairs to the computer room.

While the main floor was as glitzy as anything Jay Gatsby might have cooked up, the lower floor was paved in concrete. Here were closets full of old printers, defunct computers, outdated card catalogues, mops and cleaning fluid, paper towels and toilet paper. There was a dark room filled with cardboard boxes of old documents that I was told had come from the old library and had yet to be unpacked and sorted through. It was down here that the IT office of Ellen's fiancé Eddie was located, as well as the research department.

I entered the access code and tooled around until I found the stories I wanted. It was well after ten when I found a treasure trove, all with ominous headlines.

PILGRIM'S LANDING'S OWN MARNA VAN DUGAN FEARED DROWNED

BOAT BELONGING TO MARNA VAN DUGAN WASHES UP IN SANDS END

INCLEMENT WEATHER HINDERS SEARCH FOR MARNA VAN DUGAN

And there, on the front page of one, was a photo of Messi, hair in a ponytail, chest bare, standing at the wheel of a fishing boat. Under his photo was the quote: "I'll find her. If she's out there, I will find her and bring her back!"

The rest of the stories revealed that neither he nor anyone else had been able to find her or her body.

All this thinking had suddenly made me very thirsty, and I walked down the corridor to the bathroom for a drink of cold water. The bathroom was right next to Ellen's boyfriend Eddie's office, and I was surprised to see the light still on. He was sitting, kind of slumped over at his desk and I had a sudden, gut feeling that something was wrong.

Ellen had said she could smell a storm coming. New York City had taught me how to smell danger.

I went back to Winston's office. It was unlocked. I knew that he frequently slept at his desk, but tonight his office was empty. I grabbed a hardcover copy of *Moby Dick* off the closest shelf and returned to Eddie's office. The book might not be as effective as a stiletto-heeled shoe for bringing down an enemy, but it was better than nothing.

I peered into the darkness.

Why hadn't I taken a flashlight? I almost tripped over a wastebasket in the hallway.

I tightened my grip on *Moby Dick*.

As I came up on Eddie's office, I saw him through the glass door, he was still in the same position, slumped over his computer, as if asleep. I tried the door, but it was locked. That's when I saw it, what I had only sensed before: a pool of red blood dripping off the edge of his desk onto the concrete floor.

I screamed, though I knew nobody could hear me. The library was constructed with sound-dampening panels—plus, it was well after closing time.

The fact that the blood not yet coagulated meant that the killer was still probably nearby.

Trembling, legs wobbly, I pulled myself up the stairs, gripping the banister as tightly as I could with one hand—the other still raised above my head, carrying the hefty volume of *Moby Dick*. At my desk, I exchanged *Moby Dick* for a pair of scissors, then picked up the phone and dialed 911.

Should I get under the desk? That seemed so undignified. If I were going to be murdered, at least let me try not to die a coward.

Several excruciating minutes later, punctuated by the sound of my jagged breathing, I heard a sharp rap on the door and a loud voice called out, "Police! Open the door!"

No loud siren. No screeching of breaks. Not even a rotating light! All I could see out the plate glass were two large men.

"How do I know you're the police?" I yelled.

"Because I say so," a loud voice thundered. "What idiot locked the door?"

That sounded like a cop. I unlocked the door, and the two men quickly stepped inside.

Both wore street clothes, and while one wore a badge, the other carried a gun which he pointed in several directions before yelling, "Turn on the damn lights!"

I flicked the switch.

The man with the gun looked me over carefully.

"You're the new assistant librarian from New York. Miss... Miss...."

"Nussbaum."

"Sheriff Bill Bronson. What the hell's going on here?"

I explained what I had seen and walked reluctantly back downstairs, flanked by the sheriff and a muscled guy with the squashed nose of a boxer, wearing a badge.

It didn't take Sheriff Bill Bronson and his deputy long to break open the door to the locked IT room.

As soon as he saw the body, Bronson took out his phone and called for backup while the squashed-nose guy felt for a pulse.

Although I was still shaking, the presence of the police was a small comfort. I'd never seen a dead body before, at least not one who'd been murdered. And Ellen! My best friend, Ellen! She didn't yet know that the love of her life was gone! Her dreams of her life together with Eddie gone... Through my tears I could see that a couple of his fingers were stained with ink, and he was still wearing his watch.

But the sheriff's actions struck me as strange. He started opening drawers in Eddie's desk and rifling through papers. It seemed to me he managed to slip a couple of them into Eddie's briefcase, which was resting on the floor, but it was hard to tell because his deputy blocked my view.

"Wait!" I called out. "What if there are fingerprints or something?"

"Now Miss Nusshelm, is it? Thank you so much for your help. I'm sure you are going to be a real asset to this community."

"It's Nussbaum."

"Isn't that what I said?"

He took my arm and walked me towards the broken door.

"My deputy here will be happy to see you home."

Just then, a couple of tall men wearing jeans and sweatshirts walked through the door. The Sheriff dropped my arm, mumbled a few things to them, and took a few photos with his iPhone. The two men picked Eddie up, stuffed him into a body bag, and carried him out.

At that point, Mr. Squashed Nose took hold of my arm and deposited me inside the squad car like an escaped prisoner. When I tried to make conversation, the deputy just bit his lip and kept driving. Was he scared to talk to me because I was a Jew? A city person? Or was he scared to talk to anyone? Could he talk at all? Up close, he was less frightening. I actually felt a little sorry for him when he smiled at me and opened up the glove compartment, offering me a stick of gum. I accepted, and he drove up the road to the bungalow I had rented.

The phone was ringing when I got home. Ellen.

"I hate to bother you so late," she said, "but Eddie didn't show up for our date. He's never been late before, and he's not at home—I checked." She sounded upset.

That was when the horror of the whole situation hit me, and I threw up on the kitchen floor.

Since there was nobody else to give Ellen the bad news, it was up to me to tell her.

Chapter Two

"Consider the subtleness of the sea; how its most dreaded creatures glide under water, unapparent for the most part, and treacherously hidden beneath the loveliest tints of azure. Consider also the devilish brilliance and beauty of many of its most remorseless tribes, as the dainty embellished shape of many species of sharks. Consider, once more, the universal cannibalism of the sea; all whose creatures prey upon each other, carrying on eternal war since the world began."

—**Herman Melville**, *Moby Dick*

"Bill Bronson, you get that photographer out of here this minute!"

Letitia Rose Jefferson, the head librarian, my CEO, stood in front of the library check-out desk, hands on hips.

She was a large, imposing woman with beautiful honey-colored skin who traced her ancestry back to Thomas Jefferson himself.

Ellen had told me there was a colony of people of color who had lived on the East End of Long Island who went back almost as far the pilgrims themselves. Letitia Rose Jefferson was one of them. Pilgrim's Landing royalty. And she was not about to let anyone forget it.

"Oh, come on, Letty. It's not every day we have a murder in our town."

Bronson, wearing his sheriff's badge on a checked shirt, looking like someone from an old western except for a baseball hat, which featured a pilgrim woman, on his shaved head, put his face close to mine, while a skinny kid with stringy black hair who looked about 18, blinded me with a series of flashbulb close-ups.

"And you, Miss Nussbaum," Letitia Rose moved her leonine head in my direction. "This is a library, not a movie set".

I wriggled out from under Bronson's arm and put my glasses back on, while Bronson gave the photographer one more broad grin.

"And you, Russel Hawkeye Jones. The last time you set foot in this library was in the third grade and you never returned the book you borrowed!"

Hawkeye mumbled, "Sorry Miss Jefferson," and beat a hasty retreat towards the men's room.

Then Letitia turned to the mob of people—mob might be a bit of an exaggeration–but there were at least 25 people, some in their bathing suits and flip-flops, crowded in front of the front desk.

"Those of you with library cards form a line to your right."

"Young man!" she motioned to a tall guy with blond hair. "We don't allow flip-flops in here." She pointed to a sign on the wall.

PROPER ATTIRE REQUIRED: NO BATHING SUITS, FLIP-FLOPS, PORTABLE RADIOS, FOOD OR DRINK (EXCEPT WATER)

"The rest of you who desire a Pilgrim's Landing library card may form a line to the left to fill out an application. Proper ID with photo and local address are required."

With those words most of the crowd dispersed, a number to the ice cream store across the street, while the rest got in their cars and drove away. There was only so much energy they were willing to spend on seeing a building where a murder had taken place, especially when the sun was shining outside.

"And you," Letitia pointed to a young woman holding a baby and munching on a cookie. "Is that a Girl Scout Cookie?"

"Yes Ma'am" she answered. "Got it right outside."

"Okay, then." Letitia said. "Girl Scout cookies are allowed."

Sure enough, one glance out the plate-glass window showed me there were two tables of baked goods under a hastily scribbled sign that read:

PILGRIM'S LANDING GIRL SCOUT DEN #5 / BAKE SALE, PILGRIM'S LANDING ELEMENTARY SCHOOL

A woman in a girl scouts' uniform was busily making change, while next to her, another woman, wearing a white tennis dress, cut up slices of pie. Fresh peach, if I was right about the aroma wafting in through the open door.

Even when Barney the bookie, the back-elevator man's brother, was found knifed in the basement of my coop, more respect was paid.

"Buck up, girl," Letitia instructed. "Sometimes you got to know how to make the best of a misfortune. People like me have been doing it since Columbus arrived."

She looked down at a large, unopened box of books that had been delivered earlier in the day.

"Stop staring at the ceiling and make yourself useful. Open this box and put the new books on the shelves."

I tugged the box to a better position, then saw a flash of gray as a rat ran out and disappeared under the desk.

As a city girl, who jogged daily around the reservoir in Central Park, I was well acquainted with rats. They didn't scare me nearly as much as large bugs, and I didn't want to start a riot in the library, so I whispered to Letitia Rose. "I just saw a rat—and I have noticed a couple of the books on the back stacks seem a little tattered around the edges—is there an exterminator I can call?"

Letitia Rose glared at me. "There are no rats in Pilgrim's Landing. Everyone knows that. Perhaps a small field mouse from the wild strawberry fields across the road. I'll attend to it. You need to attend to this carton of books."

I grabbed a pair of scissors from the desk and tried to open the box, while Letitia Rose scowled and shook her head.

"You'll never get anywhere with a scissors!"

She reached into a cubbyhole behind the desk I didn't even know was there and took out a purse the size of a shopping bag, extracting from it a large pocketknife. In one motion, she opened the knife and slit through the tape on the carton. Then she expertly closed the knife against her thigh and threw it back into her purse, which she put back behind the desk. Walking over to a long oak reading table, she sat down next to an elderly woman with a cane who was reading through a copy of *The New York Times*.

I knew I still had a lot to learn about the library and the people in town, but one thing that I did know—my good friend Ellen Hinkley was devastated by Eddie's murder. I didn't know Eddie very well, but I was close to Ellen and her pain was palpable to me.

It was Ellen, after all, who had rescued me following a run of bad luck. I'd recently divorced my banker husband Murry-the-Mistake (the less said about him the better), after finding him in bed with the bartender—excuse me—the "mixologist" from the French Bistro around the corner. I'd lost my job in publishing due to a merger, and I'd recently wrecked my BMW, crashing it into a bus.

Which, I suppose, served me right for buying a German car. Never forget—except when buying a fabulous car.

Ellen had called to wish me a happy birthday the day the cast came off my broken arm, and when she heard my tale of woe, made the offer of a low-rent bungalow in Pilgrim's Landing where I could restore both body and spirit.

So I headed out for the territory, like Huck Finn, hoping to find a simpler, more satisfying life in smalltown America.

I had a therapist who once told me it was useless to try to find geographical solutions to personal problems, because "wherever you go, there you are," but just trading in my car (even if not by choice) for a bike, made me feel a hell of a lot better.

I also rediscovered my love of books (with the time to read them), and I took a couple of courses at the local college in library science, landing a job as an assistant librarian, right next to my friend Ellen.

The murder had taken place three days ago now, and after the call in which I had to break the terrible news to her about Eddie, we hadn't talked again. Not that I hadn't tried. She just wasn't answering her phone.

So I'd learned two important things about Pilgrim's Landing:

People valued their privacy; and life was not pure and simple.

I hadn't had to tell Letitia Rose what happened. She had her own channels to news. She'd phoned me at 7 a.m. the next morning to announce that the library was closed "out of respect for Edmund Roland Smith, who was not only a valued employee but a scion of one of Pilgrim's Landing's oldest families."

Today, the library was open for business again, and it was already turning out to be a very busy day. If there were no rats in Pilgrims Landing, there could certainly be no murders.

There had to be business as usual.

The rules and rhythms of everyday life restored.

I was furiously stamping books at the check-out desk when one of the tallest men I had ever seen approached the desk.

He leaned toward me, pushed back a lock of silver-gray hair, and extended his hand, although he addressed his remarks to Letitia Rose.

" Letitia Rose Jefferson, am I correct in concluding that this lovely young woman is the heroine who found poor Eddie?"

Did Letitia's golden cheeks suddenly glow, a living manifestation of her middle name?

"Now, Thomas George Halscy, you stop trying to turn the heads of my staff. It's hard enough to find anyone these days more interested in books than Hollywood movies, so you just leave her alone."

The tall man grinned. "Anyone 'round here likes words, I count my friend. I trust you're familiar with *The Pilgrim's Landing Star?*" He pointed to the rack nearby holding the local newspapers. "Think you'll enjoy tomorrow's front page—you'll be on it."

Since my most heroic act had been to accidentally discover a murder victim, I couldn't quite bask in the glory this person was trying to confer on me. More to my liking was his "lovely young woman" line, since I was pushing 45 from the wrong side. It had been a while since anyone had called me young. Lovely was in the eye of the beholder, and some of my guy-friends had given me that. My figure was still good; my salt and pepper hair had a natural gray streak inherited from my dad—and I had green eyes inherited probably from some Viking who raped one of my ancestors long ago.

But before I could shake his hand, he withdrew it and turned to Letitia.

"Letitia Rose Jefferson, may I ask you to please refrain from terrifying my photographer? He's just a boy, after all, and someone in town has given him a job. A job he's good at—if some people would just give him a chance."

And with that, he turned on his heel and left.

Which meant I didn't get to shake his hand.

Letitia Rose Jefferson neither.

***

The library copy of *The Pilgrim's Landing Star* was leaning against the front door the next morning when I arrived to open up, and sure enough, there I was, in the grip of Sheriff Bronson, looking like a wide-eyed and scared rabbit.

The actual description of the event was much shorter than the space given to the photos. There was, happily, only the one shot of me. The rest showed the sheriff sitting at his desk beneath a banner of the Pilgrim's Landing football team, The Buffalos, and a photo of Bill and Hillary Clinton, who had attended the county horse show several years ago.

A companion piece was headlined:

Edmund Roland Smith: In Memoriam

Edmund Roland Smith Jr., 42, was found murdered Monday. A native of Pilgrim's Landing, Smith was found in front of his computer by Miss Sandra Nussbaum, the new assistant librarian.

"Edmund was an important member of our team, here at Pilgrim's Landing library," said head librarian Letitia Rose Jefferson. "His gentle manner, welcoming smile and dedication to helping the entire community understand the most recent technology will be much missed by all."

"That killer will rue the day he ever came to the East End of Long Island," promised Sheriff Bill Bronson.

*Edmund is survived by his cousin Abigail Thayer Hilton, residing in Pleasant
Valley, California.*

*A memorial service will be held at The Olde Presbyterian Church, 18 Grateful
Path, Pilgrim's Landing, on Sunday, July 24.*

I searched in vain for more details about the murder. There was no mention
of cause of death. All I knew was there was a lot of blood. That ruled out stran-
gulation and poison. Had he been shot? Stabbed? Were the police deliberately
being cagey in order to trap the killer? The whole event seemed so...out of place.
Why would someone break into a library? I remembered that Eddie was still
wearing his watch. Clearly, the motive was not robbery. The only reason I could
think of that someone would break into a library late at night would be that the
person really needed a bathroom—or—a book!

I suddenly remembered the handsome Messi who pounded on the library
door after closing time.

Not that anybody would kill for a copy of *Moby Dick*...unless it was a very
special edition.

I pictured that musty-smelling room filled with cartons of old manuscripts
next door to Winston's office.

Winston had told me some of those documents were very valuable. Was there
some valuable manuscript or book stored somewhere in the library worth killing
for?

And then Winston, the head of the research department, came up to the desk.

"My dear girl! How perfectly awful for you! To be all alone like that. I feel so
guilty not being in my office when you needed me!"

Winston Worthington Fowl was one of those three-named pilgrim people
who really looked the part. He even kept a copy of his original land-grant tacked
up over his desk. He wore a bowtie and white shirt, a vest filled with strange
pins and medals, and high leather boots even in the middle of summer. His long
white hair stuck out in odd directions from under a dark cap.

Even when completely sober, Winston was not that steady on his feet. I
assured him that the copy of *Moby Dick* I borrowed from his shelves was all the
help I needed.

And then Job Abraham Farrington wheeled up to the desk. Same group of pilgrims—very different descendant.

Job must have signed up with the marines to fight in Afghanistan with the same fervor I imagine his ancestors brought to combatting the British during the American Revolution. He returned home in a wheelchair.

I knew that his family owned land all over the island, but Job, for his part, no longer seemed interested in business. He told me that his great grandfather had been a friend of William Merritt Chase and had produced a few landscapes that weren't half bad. Job had dabbled in painting, himself. The light out here on the East End had turned lots of people into Sunday painters. So when Job came back from the war, he opened an art and photography store on Main Street and volunteered to run the children's library.

To me, he was a real hero.

He rolled up to the desk, the muscles in his strong arms stretching his white t-shirt tight.

"Wanted to get here early to lay out the paints. The kids must really be freaked out by all this." He pointed to the front page of the newspaper. "Must have been awful for you. All alone like that. I'm so sorry."

He squeezed my hand.

"Hope God blesses you with only good things going forward."

I thanked him and was just logging into my computer when the janitor, Pepe, a short, quiet man from somewhere south of the border, approached the desk.

He stood in front of me holding his mop straight up, like a spear.

Although my North of the Border Spanish, learned in Brooklyn many years ago, is somewhat limited, I was determined to do my best.

Many of the mostly Mexican workers, whom I saw lined up each morning in front of the all-night Blessed Point Diner looking for day work, were gardeners, cooks, janitors, even security guards—whatever work they could find that didn't require English language skills. But their kids—wow. Totally different story. They were super All-American from the time they entered kindergarten.

I didn't know Pepe—or his kids, if he had any—but I was prepared to do my best to help him find the book of his choice.

"*Buenos dios*, Pepe. *Ayudar*? *Quiere un libro*? Me show you *donde mirar*."

I figured I'd get him hooked on a book first, then I would help him fill out the information to get a card. It had been my experience that the few adult Mexican people who ventured into the library were frightened of official looking documents.

Pepe shook his head and moved the mop a little to the right. He moved his bucket filled with water to the side and bent over the desk.

"*Mal Hombre*! *Muerte Eddie*. Eddie *amigo*."

He put his hand in his pocket and took out a small silver cross. He kissed it and put it on the desk in front of me.

"*Para usted*. *Usted* wear. No get hurt."

Then he turned, picked up his pail and his mop and headed for the stairs that led to the lower level.

Two people had already blessed me, and it was still pretty early in the morning. I didn't find these blessings comforting. On the contrary, to require so much supernatural attention seemed to suggest that some people thought I was in danger.

I kissed the cross and put it in my purse. I looked up towards the hand-blown glass chandelier hanging from the ceiling. You could never tell what kind of Gods or spirits might be flying around up there. I would take any help I could get.

When I looked up again, I found myself staring directly into the blue-green eyes of Pilgrim's Landing's own Neptune, Messi the Fisherman.

"Now, didn't I warn you to be careful the other night? You New Yorkers think you know everything. Listen to me, the only difference between that place and this one is that danger doesn't look the same or smell the same—but don't let that fool you. You shouldn't be alone after hours in this place."

The only danger I could think of at the moment involved falling for this guy.

"Ellen is usually around to keep me company."

As if the sound of her name had suddenly summoned her, Ellen walked through the door and slid quickly behind the desk.

I put my arm around her. "How are you doing? I thought you were taking the week off."

Ellen shook her head. "I couldn't stand being alone anymore. Decided I'd be better off here." She nodded at Messi.

Messi bent over the desk. "So sorry, Ellen. Eddie was a good guy. Can't make sense of a thing like this. People do things like this... they'll be caught, I know it."

"Just like you knew you'd find Marna Van Dugan."

Messi's mouth tightened.

"That's a low blow."

"Sometimes low things happen. Even in Pilgrim's Landing."

I could see Messi doing his best to let it go. It was obvious Ellen was in pain. We watched her

turn on her computer. From what I could see, there were a bunch of messages from well-wishers. She turned her attention to answering them.

Although it had only been a couple of days since I'd seen her, Ellen looked thinner and paler, a shadow sitting dutifully at her computer. My heart ached for her. I wanted desperately to go over to her desk and embrace her again. But I kept my distance, respectful of her privacy.

Messi turned his attention back to me, straightening up to his full height. He was well over six feet, with that fresh, slightly salty scent, those amazing blue-green eyes, that crooked, mischievous grin. It was the grin of someone born to break the rules. Neptune. All he needed was a trident.

"Now, that," he said, plunking down *Moby Dick* in front of me, "is what I consider a good read. A real tale of adventure. There was only one very important thing missing."

"What was that? Were there any other pages torn out? I promise you, I will find the culprit and confiscate his library card!"

Messi smiled. "No, all the pages were intact. But there are no *women* in that book! No women at all. No love. No romance. Now, I ask you, Miss Librarian—Sandy—why do you think that was?"

Suddenly my day was getting much brighter. Maybe the blessings were beginning to work.

"Maybe Melville was reluctant to discuss sailors' activities when they came to port. It was bad enough he was challenging the conventional view of God. The book was banned in its day. Probably right here at Pilgrim's Landing."

"Not everyone takes Pilgrim's Landing bans that seriously. Right now, I've got to go out and catch me some fish, but later tonight, after the library closes, maybe you and me could swap some trade secrets. I can tell you something about banned behavior in the East End, and you can tell me more about banned books."

Then he took my hand and held on to it long enough to make my day.

Unfortunately, this mood of euphoria did not last very long, because the ringing phone summoned me. Sheriff Bill Bronson.

"Hello there, Miss...Neisman. Glad to find you at your post. Seems you are as dependable as Letitia herself—though a lot prettier."

"It's Nussbaum."

"Nussbaum—isn't that what I said? Now—I need a little help from you, Miss Nussbaum. You people have a reputation—well-earned, I must say—for book learning and smarts. Problem we're facing, there's a murderer loose out there.... It's not good for business, my dear woman. Not good at all. This is high season here in Pilgrim's Landing. We can't afford to lose our tourist crowds to places like Bliss Bay, where the so-called celebs hang out, seducing people with their phony Film Festival, or, worse, to that cheesy low-class Sands End."

I decided not to react to his "you people" remark, or him calling Sands End low class (especially since I now had a date with one of their most illustrious fishermen). Instead, I politely said, "How can I help you?"

"I need you to come down my office. After all, you're the person who discovered poor Eddie. So, there are some things we need to talk about."

I wondered why it had taken the sheriff almost a week to ask me for a statement.

I was about to find out.

###

"Now you sit right there, my pretty little lady," Bill Bronson directed me to a hard-backed chair alongside a metal table that looked like it had come from the school gym.

"Can I get you some iced tea or cold water to drink?"

I shook my head.

Bronson seated himself on the edge of the table, dangling his feet close to mine.

"Now, can you tell me what brought you down to the lower level after hours last Thursday night?"

"I was doing research in the computer room. And I passed by Eddie's office on my way to get a drink at the water fountain. He looked odd, like he was asleep at his desk, but I was thirsty, so I didn't stop to check in on him at that point."

"And at what time was that?"

"It must have been just a little after ten because I had been looking at some old newspapers...."

"Why were you looking at old newspapers at ten at night?"

Something told me that Messi and Bill Bronson probably hated each other.

I cleared my throat. "I was trying to get more of a handle on the history of Pilgrim's Landing. I love the library. I love books. My house is small and dark—and lonely. I was in no hurry to go home."

"You're in the old Jensen house on Frogs Neck Road?"

I nodded. Did Frogs even have necks? What did I know—I was a city girl. But Bronson surely already knew where I lived. His deputy had driven me home.

"Old man Jensen used to volunteer for the fire department. Worked the hoses and the ladders. Good man."

Bronson edged closer, lowering his face closer to mine. "So, you're sure you didn't see Winston hanging about?"

I shook my head. "All the lights were out downstairs. I know because I almost tripped over a mop and pail the janitor had left near the staircase. Anyway, I went into Winston's office and grabbed a heavy book in case I needed to protect myself. I just had an odd feeling. It was creepy downstairs alone. Winston wasn't there."

"And when you reached the door of Eddie's office on your way back, what did you do?"

I didn't want to cast my mind back to the moment of discovery. I could feel my palms grow sweaty at the mere thought of it.

"The light was on. I looked through the glass door and I could see him slumped over his computer. I was still thinking that maybe he'd fallen asleep. But Ellen had told me they had a date that evening, so I wanted to wake him up. I tried the door, but it wouldn't open. I'm a little nearsighted. That's when I saw the blood dripping on the floor and started screaming."

"But of course nobody heard you. Everyone else had gone home."

"Yes. So that's when I went upstairs and called the police."

Bronson put up his hand. I could see he was getting a little bored with all this questioning.

"Let's skip to after I came, and we opened the door to Eddie's office. What did you see at that point?"

I fidgeted in the chair. I found it odd that he was asking me what I'd seen and not what happened. I assumed that's what he meant to ask. "I showed him where I found Eddie slumped over his computer. Your deputy took his pulse. You took a couple of photos with your iPhone. Then two guys came in with a body bag and stuffed poor Eddie inside..."

Bronson winced. "Stuffed, is not exactly what we do, Miss Nussbaum. The body was placed carefully inside the bag."

"If you say so."

"And then what did you see?"

Again, that phrasing. I had seen Bill Bronson open Eddie's desk drawer. I had seen him remove a couple of files.

It suddenly occurred to me that this entire "interview" was to make sure I had *not* seen him do that.

"The next thing I remember is that you were kind enough to ask your deputy to drive me home. That was a blessing. I was a wreck."

Bill Bronson smiled broadly and moved his body off the table.

He went back to his desk and handed me a carefully typed document.

"I think you will find most of the questions and your answers summarized here. I just need a signature."

I glanced quickly through the document he handed me. It was several pages long.

He handed me a pen.

I held the pen in the air for a few seconds, then I handed it back to him.

There it was again. That city-bred sense of danger. Unlike Ellen, I couldn't smell a storm coming, but I could smell the stink of a bad cop.

"Thanks for writing out this statement," I told him. "I'll return it to you as soon as I've had a chance to read it."

I got up and walked toward the door. But Bronson charged ahead of me.

"There are just a couple of other things before you leave. We'll need a sample of your DNA and a record of your fingerprints."

He walked back to his desk and pressed a button. His trusty deputy appeared.

"Am I a suspect?" I asked.

Bronson smiled. "My dear young lady, in my book, everyone is guilty until proven innocent."

That's not quite what I learned in school—but then I hadn't grown up in Pilgrim's Landing.

CHAPTER THREE

My father's people say that at the birth of the sun and of his brother the moon, their mother died. So the sun gave to the earth her body, from which was to spring all life and he drew forth from her breast the stars, and the stars he threw into the night sky to remind him of her soul.

—**James Fenimore Cooper**, *The Last of the Mohicans*

At 5:30, after everyone had gone, Messi rapped on the library door. I'd given up hope of his arrival, but since students gave a professor half an hour before they split, I figured I would hang out.

"Sorry! So sorry! The tide waits for no man. And I was going against it. My boat, she got knocked around a bit. Had a little trouble bringing her in."

He handled the heavy library door as if it were made of paper mache.

It did seem like a waste of time to lock the door when someone like Messi could seemingly and effortlessly blow it down. He touched my arm, his hand warm through the fabric of my blouse. At the bottom of the steps, he stooped to pluck a yellow wildflower from the ground, then handed it to me with the slightest of bows.

I tucked it into the buttonhole of my blouse. I could see he was a man who knew how to please a woman, and so I asked him, playfully, why sailors always referred to ships as "She."

"Oh, Miss Librarian, that's an easy one. Sailors love their ships. Their lives and livelihood depend on her. But she can be fickle, undependable, unpredictable. Just when you need her most, she'll disappoint you."

"And those are feminine characteristics?"

Messi smiled. "What would you say?"

"Maybe that's why there are no women in *Moby Dick*. There are hardly any women in *Huck Finn*, or *The Last of the Mohicans* either. They're all male bonding stories. There's an essay by the critic Leslie Fiedler, 'Come Back to the Raft, again, Huck Honey,' that says it all."

"Are you telling me these guys were gay? Not that I have anything against gays. After sleeping in the woods or hunting whales on the sea long enough, I suppose anything human looks good."

I shook my head. "These tales are pre-sexual, or asexual. Like when guys play soccer or baseball or something. They just bond. Maybe like when women go shopping together. It's not sexual—it's something else."

"Let's try some male-female bonding over a couple of beers." He steered me down the street to a small bar called Mohicans.

Now, I've been in a number of bars in my life. I would say there are men's bars and women's bars. There are also upscale bars in restaurants tended by female "mixologists." I could call them something else, but would rather not get stuck on that subject.

Women's bars usually have small, cozy-looking tables with a candle or flower. The aroma is more of wine than beer.

Men's bars specialize in very large TVs playing some sport you have absolutely no interest in whatsoever, like rugby—or car races. Also, men's bars are usually filled with men. One might think that these men would be eager to talk to a woman, but the truth is, most of them are there to escape from women, often a particular woman, more often than not their wife. In any case, they are much more interested in drinking and watching whatever sport is on the TV, and so, if you came in for companionship and conversation, forget it, you're better off picking up a bottle of vodka at Conscience Cove, and going home.

Mohicans was clearly a men's bar—which is why I had never entered it. Messi, on the other hand, was greeted like a long-lost frat brother.

"Hey, dude!" the bartender called out. "Good to see ya back here!"

"You, too," Messi threw back. He turned to me. "What'll you have?"

I really wanted a vodka and tonic, but if Messi was drinking beer, I would drink beer. I ordered a Guinness, which I hoped would prove I was a worthy mate. We found a rather sticky table in the back, away from the TV screens.

A skinny girl with long black hair, wearing black tights, made her way over to us and threw her arms around Messi.

"Where have *you* been?"

"Good to see ya, girl!" Messi said, unwinding himself from her embrace. "How's your ma?"

"'Bout the same. Thanks for asking."

She produced a dirty-looking cloth and wiped off the top of our table. Then she took our drink orders and left.

"The waitress," I said. "Is she Native American? The Shinnecock were here before the pilgrims, right?"

"That's what they taught us in school. Said they helped the pilgrims, gave them corn to plant. That was a mistake. Probably should have cut their throats and sunk their ships. Did you ever hear the expression, 'No good deed goes unpunished?'"

I nodded. "But they're still here. I haven't seen their reservation, but I know they have festivals and try to keep the culture alive. The library sponsors Native American dance classes."

"Right. Like the Germans have monuments for the Jews. A bit too late."

"You can't roll back history," I said. "All you can do is try to treat everyone better today. I imagine many of the Shinnecock have left, intermarried, become part of the larger society. Like that photographer kid. Hawkeye something."

"It's not as easy to reinvent yourself here as it is in New York City. People here have long memories."

I looked around. A few of the men at the bar turned to look at us. One saluted.

Messi moved his chair a little closer to me. "Are you hungry? This place has the best mussels in town."

Just what I was afraid of. Fish was bad enough. But shellfish? Shrimp, maybe. "I'm a meat and potatoes gal," I said. "Do you think they could make me a meatball hero?"

"This is Pilgrim's Landing, darling. We eat fish here."

"I thought the pilgrims ate turkeys. "

"That was just a rumor made up by the Indians. If you live here, you've got to learn to eat local."

"How about a shrimp cocktail?"

Messi just scowled and shook his head.

When the waitress returned with our beers, she announced the dinner choices: "It's mussels, clams or oysters. Mussels in garlic or tomato sauce, clams, and raw oysters."

Messi ordered mussels in tomato sauce. He reached over and took my hand. "Now, Miss Librarian, you remember our deal? I was going to tell you about Pilgrim's Landing and you were going to tell me about books? Well, your first lesson in Pilgrim's Landing—learning to eat mussels."

"How about French fries?" I asked the waitress.

She smiled. "We have French fries."

"That's what I'll have."

"We'll share," Messi said, smiling.

I felt like a kid whose parents were trying to get me to eat my spinach. Was I going to let this guy bully me? I'd been in a marriage with a man who, as a financial advisor, had made his living telling people what to do. I'd had a relationship with a homicide cop who made his living dictating the rules to others. I hadn't given an inch to either of them. This guy had a lot to learn about his librarian.

Nevertheless, I clinked glasses with him and found myself unable to resist returning his smile. Guinness for courage. I think I saw a poster once with that on it.

He took my hand, and I looked into those turquoise eyes again. A mistake because I very quickly began to think that eating a mussel might not be such a bad idea after all.

In my sternest voice, I said, "Please cut the Miss Librarian stuff. My name is Sandra. My friends call me Sandy."

"I'll remember that. Now Sandy, about those mussels...."

I shook my head.

When they arrived, I'll admit they smelled good. The French fries, on the other hand, were a little limp.

"Try one," Messi urged, reaching into the bowl and holding out a glistening black shell.

I shook my head.

"I'll give you twenty dollars to eat this mussel."

"Not happening."

Messi picked the horrid orange-yellow glob out of the shell with a three-pronged fork and dangled it in front of me.

"Fifty!"

I laughed. "You think I have a price?"

Messi smiled and shrugged, continuing to dangle the mussel in front of me. "We're still talking about seafood, aren't we?"

"I sure hope so."

"Just so you know, I've never had to pay for sex. At least, not in cash."

He opened his mouth and slid the wretched mussel in with the fork. Some of the sauce dripped down his chin. His turquoise eyes glowed. It brought to mind Allen Bates eating a fig in the movie version of D.H. Lawrence's *Women in Love*, one of the sexiest, most scandalous scenes in the history of cinema.

Messi licked his lips. He held up another mussel in front of me.

"Come on. I'll feed it to you. You'll love it. "

I shook my head. "Another time. It's too soon."

Messi's piercing eyes dared me to resist him. Luckily, a familiar voice called out—"Messi! God help us, you're back!"—forcing us to break eye contact as Job propelled his wheelchair right up to our table.

Messi stood to greet him, the two embracing like long-lost best buddies. It was a surprise to me. They seemed so different. Job, a pilgrim person with three names, an aristocratic native of Pilgrim's Landing, and Messi, a descendant of immigrants, an outsider and relative newcomer. One was dark with long hair pulled back in a mini-pony tail; the other seated in a wheelchair, his blond, closely cropped hair giving him the air of a soldier. Yet seeing them together, their friendship made some sense. Both radiated a kind of strength—the muscles in their chest and arms clearly showing through their t-shirts. They would either be friends—or arch enemies.

"I was going to ask what brought you back, but I think I can see for myself," Job said, and here he cast a brief glance at me, before looking back at Messi. "It's been a while, hasn't it?"

Did I imagine, in Job's question, an allusion to Messi's last girlfriend? Not a subject conducive to new beginnings. I took another swallow of my Guinness and tried to pretend I wasn't there.

"It's time," Messi said, as if he could read my mind. "Life goes on."

I hoped Messi wouldn't invite Job to join us. I was looking forward to being alone with him.

Maybe he was thinking the same thing. At any rate, he didn't offer Job an invitation.

Another shake of hands, a few more good-to-see-ya's, and Job rolled out of the bar.

"I didn't know you two were friends. You seem so different."

Messi picked up his beer. "We bonded over our losses."

"His legs—your girl?"

"He lost his girl, too. Used to be pretty tight with your friend Ellen. They were engaged to be married. Then he went off to war, and she found another beau with three names and two good legs."

This was a surprise to me. Ellen and I were pretty close, but she had never mentioned that there had been a thing between her and Job. Had she now lost two possible mates? One to a stray bullet in a country across the globe and another right in her hometown?

And Eddie. His rival. Job had to see him every day. See him and know he was sleeping with Ellen, while he, he... couldn't do anything about it.

I wiped beer foam from my upper lip with a fingertip. "I feel bad for both of them. Some people seem to attract bad luck."

"Not sure about the luck part. I told Job not to join up. Make love, not war, and all that. But like I said, life goes on. Still, I feel bad for him."

"It's like Jake Barnes in *The Sun Also Rises*. He's wounded in the war and can't make love to the woman he loves, Lady Brett. He has to watch her go off with the bullfighter."

"Hemingway—he was a fisherman, too, wasn't he?"

I nodded. "*The Old Man and the Sea*."

"How does that one end?"

"You need to read it."

"Spoken like a true librarian." Messi scooped out another mussel. He held it up silently in front of me before shrugging and depositing it in his mouth.

We had another couple of beers, laughed a lot, made fun of a few of the pilgrim people with three names we both knew, and then, after we finished eating and drinking, walked down the road to the bay. There was a full moon, and it glimmered on the water like a pathway to the stars. The air smelled fresh, and every once in a while, a spray of saltwater rose up in front of us like a veil, leaving behind a whiff of salt. A seagull swooped down and landed on a post nearby.

And then Messi kissed me, his mouth salty as the sea, and we sat there together, our arms around each other, staring out at the water. "Where do you live?" he whispered at last.

"Eighteen Frogs Neck Road."

"The old Jensen place?"

Of course, he knew it. Jensen had been a fisherman. Messi half-carried me to his car, parked in a wooded spot off the road, and drove me home.

He escorted me onto the porch, standing next to me while I fumbled around in my purse for the key.

"Would you like to come in?" I asked.

He took me in his strong arms, held me for a long moment, then said, "It's too soon," and walked slowly back to his car.

That night, I dreamed about the blue baby floating in a blue-green sea.

***

"Messi only knows part of the story," Ellen said when I asked her about Job. "We went out for a while, but I was never that keen on him. We were just kids. When he went off to war, I wrote to him. It seemed very romantic. But as time went by, I wrote less and less. Then, when he got wounded, I felt for him, obviously. I visited him in the hospital a couple of times after he came back.... Maybe he thought there was more feeling between us than there was. He obviously told Messi some kind of tale. Sounds like guy talk he made up. Show them he had a girl just like the rest of them. We're friends now. He certainly seems to have accepted that. He even told me how sorry he was about Eddie."

I believed what she told me. It rang true. I never felt any special connection between Ellen and Job. Messi was bringing his Italian sensibility into a situation he really knew little about.

Ellen's relationship to Job, or lack of, was in the past. Much as I cared about her, that situation wasn't my problem. My problem was dealing with a sheriff who obviously did not like me.

Since knowledge is power, after the library closed the following night, I once again stayed behind. This time I brought a good flashlight, a pair of gloves that wouldn't leave fingerprints, and a key to the new door that had been installed in Eddie's office.

I walked quietly down the stairs, careful not to fall over any cleaning equipment the janitor might have left. Winston's door was closed, the lights turned off, so I figured he had gone home—or else was fast asleep.

Yellow crime scene tape blocked the doorway to Eddie's office. For a minute, I had the urge to turn and run. The library, which at first had seemed like a safe haven for my restless soul, now seemed rife with danger. Particularly here, on the lower floor, which was half underground and quiet as a tomb.

Nevertheless, I was on a mission. I refused to chicken out now.

I carefully detached one end of the tape, inserted the key in the door, and entered.

Flicking the light on, everything looked very much as it had the night I discovered the body.

I walked over to Eddie's desk and opened the main drawer. There were a bunch of files inside. I took a quick look, but everything I saw was in some kind of computer code and I couldn't make heads or tails of it.

There was a brown stain on the floor near where Eddie's briefcase had been. At first, I figured it was dried blood. But looking closer, I could see it was a much darker stain. Was it ink?

I traced the stain up to Eddie's desk and found a similar stain on the desktop. It struck me as strange that an IT guy would use so much ink. The whole idea of technology, the internet, the computer and all that stuff, was to avoid paper and ink.

Of course, there was a printer on the desk. That took ink. I flipped open the top and looked down at the cartridge. It was intact. No ink spillage or stains.

I thought back to the last time I had seen Eddie, slumped over his desk, fingers stained with ink.

Did any of this mean anything? Did he use an ink pad the way we did upstairs, to stamp dates on the library card inserts? I opened a couple of drawers, but didn't find any ink pads.

And then I saw it—an ink bottle in the top drawer. It had been turned over and had leaked onto the floor. The label read "Indelible black ink."

I picked up the bottle and slid it into the pocket of my trousers. Then I turned off the lights. Locked the door. Replaced the police tape and walked towards the stairs. That was when I saw the janitor, Pepe, standing with his mop and staring at me as I approached. *"Buenos noches,"* I said and continued on my way up.

***

Notes from Sandra, Assistant Librarian
    Mussel: Dreissena Polymorpha
    Phylum: Mollusca
    Class: Bivalvia
    Taste: Unimaginable. Probably slimy and rubbery. To be avoided except if starving.

Chapter Four

*"You did not kill the fish only to keep alive and sell for food, he
thought. You killed him for pride and because you are a fisherman. You loved him when he was alive and you loved him after.
If you love him, it is not a sin to kill him. Or is it more?"*

—**Ernest Hemingway**, *The Old Man and the Sea*

"Thanks for stopping by." Thomas George Halsey bent his tall frame
toward me and ushered me to a large chair. There was no chance my
"sweet little ass" was going to get stuck in this one.

Up close, Thomas George Halsey looked considerably older than I thought
when I'd first seen him. Close to the age of Letitia Rose, I'd say, mid-70's. There
were lines around the corners of his eyes and the sides of his mouth, and deep
grooves in his forehead. But I could tell he'd been very handsome in his younger
days. His profile could have been on an old coin.

Everything in the office was super-big, as if I had entered the Kingdom of
Giants in *Jack and the Beanstalk*. There was a huge map of Long Island on
the wall behind an enormous desk; three overstuffed chairs—one with stuffing
spilling out from a rent in the bottom—and an enormous TV screen hanging
on the opposite wall.

On one chair, so quiet I hardly noticed him, was Russel Hawkeye Jones. He was holding a camera and had a book on his lap, but his eyes were firmly fixed on his editor.

"Call me Hal," he said, waving a hand at the boy in the corner. "And that's Russel Hawkeye Jones. Hawkeye for short."

I nodded. "Call me Ismael," I said. "I feel like a traveler in a new world."

Hal squeezed himself behind his desk and cleared a space in front of him, so he could see me more clearly.

"Ah, I hear you've already met our own not-so-ancient mariner with a tale to tell."

I'd wanted a small town, I'd gotten a small town—complete with small-town gossip, especially about the new librarian and her attachments.

"A tale to tell? Messi? He hasn't uttered a word. I read about the drowning of that girl in your *Pilgrim's Landing Star.*"

"They never did recover her body. That's what ultimately saved him."

"Saved him? I thought he was in mourning for two years."

Hal shifted some papers in front of him.

"There were a number of people in town who thought he had done away with her. It was rumored that she had another boyfriend and was going to leave him. But without a body, it was hard to make the charges stick. Messi disappeared all right, though maybe not because he was in mourning. He waited till the rumors died down before he came back."

Hearing this really knocked the breath out of me. I could understand that Messi was an outsider—someone who didn't follow the rules, but this kind of nasty gossip both offended me and shook me up. I got to my feet and stood over the desk, eyes locking with Hal's.

"You don't like Messi very much, do you?"

He shrugged. "I'm an observer. I try to report the truth as I see it. Messi was the best soccer player the East End League ever had. He has lots of friends in this town. A bunch of enemies, too. Some say he carries more than fish and tourists on his boat. Spends the winters in Key West where anything goes.

"But I didn't invite you down here to discuss Messi. I'd like to do a little personal profile on you—what brought you to Pilgrim's Landing, what your former life was like, the differences between urban life in New York City and your life here in Pilgrim's Landing. You know, the kind of thing."

He squirmed out from behind his giant desk and walked over to me, bending down to give my shoulder a squeeze.

"I like you, Sandra Nussbaum. More important, Letitia Rose likes you—and she's really hard to please. We need some new blood around here. The old blood's running out—no pun intended."

Nothing like a little flattery to mollify a person. And Hal at least remembered my name.

I pictured the pool of blood on the floor beneath Eddie's desk. I pictured Winston, drunk and asleep at his desk. Job in his wheelchair.

Yes—I would say the town badly needed a transfusion.

Halsey nodded at Hawkeye, who moved in front of me, and then from side to side, taking phony "candid" shots for his boss.

Hal sat on the edge of his desk, his long legs stretching out in front of him.

"So, what made you decide to leave the Big Apple and bless the East End of Long Island with your talents?"

The truth was, I'd been desperate to leave the home of all my failures as quickly as possible. I probably would have moved to Montana if someone had offered me a free house for the summer. But I'd give Hal what he was looking for—a PR piece to amuse his readers.

I cleared my throat. "Call it a mid-life crisis. I decided to leave my executive position and the fast-paced life in New York City for something entirely different. Plus, New York City is awful in the summer—hot and dirty. Ellen found me an inexpensive cottage to rent out here for the summer. I've always loved to swim. What could be better than diving into that gorgeous clear bay, and inhaling that fresh sea air?"

"Where did you learn to swim?" Hal asked me, while scribbling in his notebook.

"Rockaway Beach, where the waves are so big that surfers come from all over. My uncle was a fireman. He taught me how to dive through the break to reach the calm waters beyond."

This piece of news really seemed to impress Hal, who continued to scribble furiously.

I was beginning to enjoy myself. "Not only do lots of New Yorkers swim," I bragged, "some of us go on to become experts. For two years I was part of a water ballet team that went all over the East Coast performing."

Even Hawkeye was impressed by this. He lowered his camera and stared at me.

Hal jumped off the edge of the desk. "Water ballet! An assistant librarian who is practically a mermaid! No wonder you feel so at home here in Pilgrim's Landing."

He glanced once more at his notes. "And what did you do after the water ballet?"

"I was the editor-in-chief of a large publishing company, where I edited new editions of classics like *Moby Dick* and *The Last of the Mohicans* that featured new front and back material, including the latest research on the authors and the backgrounds of the stories. "

"New research? The classics are the classics. They never change. Time has shown them to be the best books, generation after generation."

I smiled. "Oh, they're still the best. Better perhaps because modern research lifted the veil of respectability a little. Modern critics have discovered that Dickens had a lifelong secret affair with a mistress who was an actress. Walt Whitman was a homosexual and...."

Hal held up his hand.

"We love the classics. Why do we need to know about the secret lives of the authors? The books speak for themselves. "

"I think it makes the authors more relatable. It shows 'The truth of the human heart.'"

"Ah! The truth of the human heart. That's Hawthorne, isn't it? You are clearly a great asset to our library and community. Never let it be said that we here at Pilgrim's Landing do not understand the truth of the human heart."

Hal closed the pad and stood up.

"You're Jewish, aren't you, Miss Nussbaum?"

"Yes, I am." I didn't like questions like this. I considered Hal an intelligent, educated person. I was ready for him to be conservative, but not an anti-Semite.

Hal approached my chair. "There's a very large synagogue on Gratitude Lane. Are you a member?"

I shook my head. "I identify myself as Jewish, as sharing in the history of the Jews. I celebrate a couple of the holidays from time to time, but I am unaffiliated with any synagogue."

"Unaffiliated! That's not a good thing in Pilgrim's Landing, Miss Nussbaum. To be unaffiliated is to be an orphan in society—swept this way and that—with no anchor, no set of values, no loyalty. Such a person does not inspire confidence."

"I may not belong to any church or synagogue, but that doesn't mean I don't have a set of values or loyalty."

"Of course not. There are many people on the East End who don't believe in any god at all—but nevertheless they belong to some church or other. It's just custom. Everyone belongs to something."

"So, as long as everything looks good, that's enough for you—for all of you?"

"I can't answer for all the East End any more than you can answer for everyone in New York City. I can only pass on what is traditional, here, what will make your life easier if you choose to remain with us. The rest is up to you."

He leaned his head close to mine, and Hawkeye took a photo.

"I'll give it some thought," I said. Smiling at Hawkeye, I added, "Thanks for making me famous." And with that, I walked out the door.

***

I had just climbed into bed when my doorbell rang.

Messi! Why not? Hope springs eternal. I quickly slipped on a white satin slip, instead of the oversize "What is Life Without Choice" t-shirt from one of my marches on Washington in the 1980s, fluffed up my hair, pinched my cheeks for a little color, and went to the door.

And there was Ellen, tears streaming down her face, her slicker fluttering around her ankles, flip-flops falling off her feet, a perfect picture of misery. She'd always had an aura of quiet dignity, keeping her deepest feelings under lock and key. Without a word, I flung my arms around her and pulled her into the kitchen.

She was shivering, although it was quite warm, and I threw a large beach towel over her shoulders and lit a fire under the kettle for a cup of tea.

"I'm so sorry," she sobbed. "I'm so sorry to bother you." She kept apologizing as I made her a cup of Jasmine tea.

"Shush! Shush now. It's no trouble." Though I was a coffee drinker myself, I always kept a few tea bags around. My mom gave me tea whenever I felt sick—and I knew that was Ellen's drink of choice.

I sat down next to her and handed her a couple of tissues along with the steeping tea.

"It's all so terrible!" she practically wailed. "The only will on record leaves everything to Eddie's cousin Abigail, who must be eighty years old. She called and asked me to handle the funeral arrangements, so I went to the funeral home yesterday to pick out a coffin and the mortician said that Eddie had already been cremated. Cremated! I had to choose a small box instead. The sheriff told him the autopsy had made a mess of things and he wanted to save the family the heartache of having to see the mutilated body."

This certainly sounded strange to me, but dead was dead, and coffin or box, Eddie was gone, and my friend Ellen was suffering.

"I just couldn't stay in that house tonight! Mom—she's had Alzheimer's for years. All day she's been crying out, Eddie! Eddie! Again and again. I called my friend Annie, who lives down the road, and she said she'd stay with her tonight. Tomorrow is Eddie's memorial, and I just had to get out of there. "

She moved her cup to the side and put her head down on her arms and sobbed.

I rubbed her shoulders and made a soothing sound. I thought about tomorrow—how the entire town would be at the Olde Presbyterian Church.

"Don't go!" I said to her. "Stay here. I'll tell them you were feeling too ill to attend. Everyone will understand. They're your friends."

I don't know if that was the absolutely right thing to say, or the absolutely wrong thing, but whatever it was, Ellen suddenly sprang to her feet, as if I'd sent a shock through her entire body.

"Of course, I'm going to Eddie's memorial service. How could you even make such a crazy suggestion?"

She moved toward me and put her hand on my shoulder. "I realize you don't understand how things are done here in Pilgrim's Landing, but I would never not go to Eddie's service. Anyway, I'd really appreciate it if I could stay the night here. I can just curl up here on the sofa."

"I'll take the sofa. You take my bed."

Ellen smiled and rubbed a knuckle on my cheek. "The sofa will be fine. There is one more thing, though, if you don't mind. Do you have anything stronger than a cup of tea?"

I smiled with understanding and poured Ellen a shot of vodka. She gulped it down like medicine, then curled up on the sofa and fell immediately asleep.

I sat up for a while, staring out the window at the stars. Without Eddie, Ellen seemed like a balloon that had lost all its air.

***

The memorial service for Edmund Roland Smith was to be held at the Olde Presbyterian Church on Gratitude Road, between Pilgrim's Landing and Bliss Bay. First established in 1640 by the pilgrims as a community meeting house, it had scarcely changed: plain white outside, plank boards on the floor, simple pew benches, even the bell, high up in the tower, dated back to the 1700s. It was a trip back to a simpler time.

I had come with the rest of the library staff: Letitia Rose Jefferson, Job Abraham Farrington, Winston Worthington Fowl, and a few of the volunteers who taught courses in English as a Second Language, organic gardening and yoga.

I liked churches, especially since I had never spent a good deal of time in synagogue—the one in Brooklyn attended by my parents being a gloomy place that smelled of stale sweat. I was a cultural Jew, not a religious one. I knew a few stories from The Old Testament: that the Jews had escaped from Egypt, were kicked out of Spain, and seemed to be outsiders in every society, but in church I felt like a real tourist, admiring the architecture and the portraits of saints without thinking about my soul. I even liked the music.

It wasn't strictly white, either. Though I didn't see any Hispanics—even Pepe had not come—there were a number of conservatively dressed African Americans—the descendants of the people of color who settled in the area hundreds of years earlier.

Letitia Rose, decked out in a white picture hat and white dress printed with rose petals, looked like the hostess of a garden party. For such a large woman, she moved gracefully and seemed comfortable with everyone and anyone. There she was chatting with Sally Brier Montgomery, the elderly lady with the cane who came almost every day to the library, and shaking hands with Thomas George Halsey, "Hal," and holding his hand longer, it seemed to me, than anyone else's. With him was that skinny Hawkeye kid—camera in hand.

Ellen, who had gone home to dress before coming, was a striking figure in a pale-yellow dress, her hair pulled back in a bun, under a small, black hat with a veil that half-covered her face, holding a leather-bound bible adorned with gold-foil lettering in her hand. She nodded and shook hands, smiled at the small children she recognized, and managed to greet almost everyone who had come to the service.

Eventually, she seated herself in the front row, alone. Apparently, the cousin from California who was to inherit the mansion on the cliff and everything else Eddie owned, had not made it to the memorial service.

In the back pew, completely ignored by Letitia and Ellen, was Sheriff Bill Bronson and the deputy with the squashed nose.

After a while, the din of voices began to settle down. The organ started up, and a chorus began to sing.

I glanced towards the doors and saw that there were many more people gathered outside—an assortment of townsfolk—the baker, the manager of the general store, the postman, a few brown-skinned people with longish, straight black hair (probably Shinnecock) and a number of other people of color. The doors remained open, and I was about to turn back toward the pulpit when I saw him—tall and muscular, hair pulled back in a knot—as he slipped inside and found a place to stand in back, leaning against the white wall of the church.

I waved, trying to catch his eye, but either Messi didn't see me or didn't want to see me.

The minister, a tall, pale gentleman in a flowing black robe with white collar, sidled up to the pulpit, opened his bible—and, in a deep, resonant voice, asked us to turn to page 87: a reading from the letter of *Saint Paul to the Romans:*

Brothers and sisters:

Are you unaware that we who were baptized into Christ Jesus were baptized into his death?

We were indeed buried with him through baptism into death,

So that just as Christ was raised from the dead

By the glory of the Father

We too might live in newness of life.

In front of me, in a small silver box, was all that remained of Edmund Roland Smith.

The minister bent over the silver box. He lit a candle on each side. He waved incense over it. The congregation dutifully followed along, intoning the words of the psalm.

When the service was over, people began filing out of their pews, mingling once again. I saw Messi heading briskly towards Ellen.

And then suddenly, a woman with gray hair rose from a middle pew and yelled out, "You!"

She pointed her finger at Messi. "You! Satan! Satan, get behind me!"

It was Sally Brier Montgomery—the widow who hung out at the library. She made a grab for the silver box filled with Eddie's ashes, as Messi, Ellen and Leticia-Rose surrounded the pedestal. The minister tried to steady the pedestal, but the box fell to the ground, the top opening and Eddie's ashes spilling to the floor.

As the entire congregation watched, a sudden breeze blew through the open door, carrying a cloud of Eddie's ashes up high to the rafters of the church, gradually dispersing out into the open air.

The gray-haired widow fell to the floor. The minister bent over her with his incense, and Messi headed towards the exit.

The sheriff stepped in front of Messi. For a moment, they stared each other down. Then the sheriff moved aside, and Messi walked out into the sun.

CHAPTER FIVE

"And then Clyde... swimming heavily, gloomily and darkly to shore. And the thought that, after all, he had not really killed her. No. no. Thank God for that. He had not. And yet... had he? Or, had he not?"

—**Theodore Dreiser**, *An American Tragedy*

I looked for Ellen as the congregation quickly emptied out from the church, but she had disappeared.

I called her several times during the hours that followed, but no one picked up, not even her demented mother or the neighbor who had been taking care of her.

I wasn't able to sleep that night. The sound of the widow's cry—as she pointed her finger at Messi and screamed, "Satan!"—kept reverberating in my ear, like an old vinyl record that had gotten stuck.

Worse, I kept picturing Messi, my Neptune, my god of the sea, as the devil, as Satan. Instead of a trident, he now held a pitchfork.

The iconography of the two was really quite similar. The ancient gods gave rise to the ones in the New Testament. Reverse the trident and you get a pitchfork.

I dragged myself to the library in the morning, still worried about Ellen and confused about my feelings for Messi. To my relief, when Ellen did finally show up, she gave my hand a squeeze as she joined me behind the desk. Still, she seemed distant, preoccupied.

"That was quite a service."

"A disservice I would say." Ellen turned her head away from me and busied herself setting up her computer. It was clear she did not want to talk about Eddie's memorial. I sat at the desk, hoping someone would call.

I fiddled with my roller-deck, sighed, and moved a stack of returned books from one side of the desk to the other. I coughed.

"What?" Ellen finally relented.

"Do many people in the area think that Messi murdered his girlfriend because she was going to leave him?"

"No. There are a number of people who believe he killed her because she was pregnant."

Pregnant! That would be a complication, but in today's world not a death sentence,

"This Marna person who disappeared. Did you know her? She grew up here in Pilgrim's Landing. What was she like?"

"She did grow up here, but she was descended from the Dutch settlers, not the pilgrims, and her family never mixed that much with the rest of us. Marna went to that fancy private school in Bliss Bay. She was pretty enough in that Dutch-girl way, blond, kind of square-looking—or at least she was until she became a heroin addict—then she just looked wasted most of the time. I don't really know what Messi saw in her except maybe they both thought of themselves as free spirits."

I wondered if her death was like a modern version of Dreiser's *American Tragedy*. Only in that story the protagonist had to get rid of the poor girlfriend because he wanted to marry the rich girlfriend. But Messi was already with the rich girl!

"If he loved her, and she was pregnant, why would he kill her? He could have just married her. It would have been much simpler."

Ellen shook her head. "You have a lot to learn about Pilgrim's Landing."

I knew enough to remember that their ancestors were the same people who burned witches in Salem. I was quite sure the entire town believed in the Devil.

Leticia-Rose had come in. She walked up to the desk and gave Ellen a hug.

"Now, you listen to me, young lady. Your Eddie's ashes have flown right out of that box, straight up to heaven. Lord have mercy on our souls! I never did see such a miracle here in our own church! You have been blessed. The entire congregation has been blessed—except, perhaps, for one person. And you should not forget that. You are young and pretty and you will have lots of love in your life."

Talk about making lemonade out of lemons. Letitia Rose was an expert.

I wondered if the "one person" not blessed in Letitia's mind was Messi or the widow.

And then Letitia turned to me.

"There are some people in this town who think that just because a man is good-looking and wears his hair in a ponytail, he's a heathen to be avoided. Only ignorant people think like that."

"So, you don't think that Messi is the Devil?"

"I gave him a library card, didn't I? And so far, he has returned all his books on time."

I wanted to ask her if he had ever taken out Dreiser's *American Tragedy*, except I didn't really want to know.

Then Job rolled up to the desk.

"Disgusting! When will people in this town wake up to the twenty-first century? "

It was the first time I saw him wearing his army jacket with his purple heart.

"The only devil I believe in is the one facing me with a machine gun."

His closely cropped hair stood up straight like rows of soldiers. He seemed to be in full battle gear.

"I'm so sorry, Ellen. "

Job turned to me. "And Messi? People here still think of him as an outsider, even though he was born and bred at Sands End. How's he feeling?"

"You'll have to ask him. I haven't talked to him since we ran into you at Mohicans."

Job picked up a copy of *Alice in Wonderland* that sat on top of the pile of books in front of me.

"This belongs in the Children's Room. I'll take it back."

I looked over at the long oak table where a skinny adolescent, who looked maybe 15 or 16, was holding a copy of *Winnie the Pooh*.

"I think that kid was reading it. I'll bring it back later."

I walked over to the kid and sat down next to him. I knew some of the young Hispanic kids who hung around the library. They often came in around lunchtime because the library provided a cheap lunch in the garden for minors. But this kid was a regular. I glanced at the name written on the card in the back of *Alice in Wonderland*. Jose Lopez. He closed the book when I approached, as if he had done something wrong. I figured he was embarrassed to be caught reading a kid's book.

"*Winnie the Pooh* is a favorite of mine, too," I told him. "It's a good way to learn English—and it's really fun."

He brushed back a strand of hair and opened the book again. He flipped through a few pages until he came to the passage he was looking for. He read: 'You can't stay in you... your... corner of the... forest waiting for others to come to you. You have to go to them... sometimes."

He turned to me. "What does that mean?"

"Well, a corner is a small space, like...." I pointed to the corner near the window, "like that and...."

Jose shook his head. "I know the words, but I don't understand what they mean. Why does he have to leave the forest?"

How to explain the psychology and philosophy of a simple idea in a kid's book to a kid from another culture? Jose was right on starting his English language education with children's books.

"The words mean that sometimes it is important to go out of your comfort zone, like, cross the street even though you are afraid of traffic—because on the other side of the street is a new adventure—or prize. Like, you may want to learn to swim, but you think your friends will make fun of you, or the lifeguard won't want to teach you, so you just stay on the beach and look at the water. That's your corner of the forest. Does that make sense?"

He still looked a little puzzled.

"Or.... Let's look at it this way. Most of the kids out here eat clams and mussels—stuff that looks really slimy and disgusting to you, but there's a little part of you that wants to be like everyone else. Soooo, your corner of the forest is really a state of mind, not an actual forest, but sometimes you need to take a chance and try something new. "

Was I talking to him or was I talking to me? Maybe everything you really needed to know in life you could find in the great books written for children.

I opened *Alice in Wonderland* and flipped through it.

"Begin at the beginning," the King said, very gravely, "and go on till you come to the end: then stop."

I smiled at Jose and flipped to another page. "Why, sometimes I've believed as many as six impossible things before breakfast."

Jose nodded his head up and down at that one.

I handed him the book. "There's lots of stuff in this book that I don't understand, myself. Why don't you stay with Winnie for a while? And if you have any questions, don't hesitate to ask me."

I walked back to the front desk and glanced at him over my shoulder. He was too small, too thin for any adolescent boy. Even from a distance, I could see the hollows in his cheeks, the faded look of his skin. Was there someone—some social services agency that looked after kids like this?

"Ellen, that kid at the far table. Do you know him?"

Ellen looked at him over the top of her computer.

"Don't know his name. He comes here a lot. Him and three or four other Mexican kids. 'Specially in the summer when they can't get free food in school. There're kids like them all over the East End. They come, work in the gardens, pick the corn. Then they leave. How did they get here? Legal, illegal? Most of the people out here follow Bill Clinton's idea for the military. Don't ask, don't tell. Social Services out here works for the taxpayers. St. Mary's Church? That big

Catholic Church in Sands End? They have some kind of soup kitchen. That's all I know. It's none of my business—and it's none of yours."

One of the phones began to ring, and then another, and then people began to line up to check out books. And just like that, I got too busy to keep thinking about either Jose or Messi.

***

After my last fateful visit to Eddie's office on the ground floor, I tried to stay out of that part of the library. It gave me the creeps. I often ate my lunch outside (whatever sandwich I had managed to throw together, or a handful of the little wild blueberries that grew everywhere, together with a few fat juicy strawberries) on the bench by the side of the road overlooking the bay. Today I felt I needed something a bit loftier. Something closer to heaven. Maybe it was Zeus I needed today, not Neptune.

There was a terrace that made a ring around the roof of the library. Ellen had told me it was called "The Widow's Walk" because that was where the sailors' wives would watch for the return of their husbands—many of whom never did return.

There was a small spiral staircase from the ground floor up to the roof. Today, the sky was a cloudless blue, and there was a gentle breeze that carried the smell of newly cut grass and sea air all the way to the front desk where I sat. It seemed as if all of nature was smiling. It was the perfect day for a roof-top picnic.

When I told Winston my plan, he shook his head. "Oh, no, my dear. That's not a good idea at all. A widow's walk is no place for a picnic. It should be called the Devil's walk. There have been some... shall we say... sightings. Strange lights... shadows. The young people think it has bad karma."

I guess I shouldn't have been surprised. If the pilgrims believed in witches, why not dead people coming back to haunt the living?

As for me, I was not buying any of it. Especially as the sun was shining. Midnight might be a different story.

So, I grabbed my cup of berries and started up the stairs.

"Miss Nussbaum! Where are you going with that cup of fruit?" Letitia Rose gave me a stern look and put her hands on her hips.

"I thought it was a perfect day for a little picnic upstairs."

"'Course you can do whatever you want, but that ring round the roof—that is *not* a picnic ground. Won't find many locals choosing to hang out up there. Bad luck place if ever there was one. Just last week, one of our visitors told me she saw her dead husband walking around up there clear as day."

"Maybe it was Hamlet's father. Do you believe in ghosts?"

Letitia Rose squeezed my shoulder. "I believe in God, Mary, Jesus and the Holy Ghost. Remember what Hamlet says to Horacio? 'There is more between Heaven and Earth than is dreamed of in your philosophy.'"

"In my pocket, I have a little silver cross that Pepe the janitor gave me, and I also recently made friends with Neptune, so I guess I have the bases covered."

All the negative talk had dampened my mood a little bit but when I pushed open the door and stepped out into the sunlight, I felt like Athena, the Goddess of Wisdom, looking over the world.

I was amazed to find the wooden walkway under my feet covered with cigarette butts, a few candy wrappers, and a small pile of polished stones.

Clearly not everyone in Pilgrim's Landing was afraid of ghosts.

From what I could see, some people came up here for a smoke in the great outdoors—and maybe had some fun seeing who could pitch a stone furthest into the bay.

I took a deep breath of the fresh, salty air. The widow's walk was made of wood but there were posts every few feet set with white marble figures. There was Athena front and center, the Goddess of Wisdom, holding a book. A few feet further on was Neptune with his trident. And who was that? I walked closer to read the metal plate on the bottom of the figure, a long-haired young girl who looked like Alice in Wonderland. Sure enough, it was! And that egg-shaped figure there? Humpty Dumpty!

I walked more quickly now. Could that figure with the halo be the Virgin Mary? Yup! And that figure on the cross, of course, was Jesus.

I looked around for Moses, but I actually had little idea of what he looked like, since Jews generally avoided representations of holy people in their synagogues. But there—that must be Shakespeare—and over there, the figure with the unkempt beard, Whitman. And that stern-faced figure, Emerson. At the far end of the walk—Pocahontas. And that tall figure in tattered clothing? Huck's friend Jim!

What a silly, crazy, wonderful mélange! The town fathers, and perhaps a mother or two, in their fierce devotion to correctness, decided to include everyone.

There were no chairs, so I sat down on an unlittered section of the walk.

The water below shimmered with gold and silver ripples in the sunlight, and far out along the horizon there was a thin line of land where the sky met the sea.

Was I looking at Connecticut, or maybe just the North Fork of Long Island? Geography was not my strong suit. No matter. I munched on a ripe strawberry and counted myself lucky to be alive.

The sun shone so brightly, I closed my eyes for a few minutes and embraced the warmth of the sun on my cheeks. Suddenly, the gentle breeze gathered enough force to send the candy wrappers skidding along the surface of the roof and blow a chill into the air. Then, a small cloud passed in front of the sun, casting shade on the rooftop as if a frown had passed over the world.

I heard the creak of the door to the stairway and, when I turned around, saw a tall, thin woman all dressed in black, wearing a bonnet that shaded her face. As my breath caught in my throat, I watched her take a couple of steps towards me, her long black skirt making swishing sounds against her bare legs.

Her arm was raised and in her gloved hand was a knife.

Was this really happening? Was it a dream? The knife definitely did not seem like it was part of a dream, the sun shining so brightly off the metal of the blade it was blinding.

I realized that I had to get away, but I was paralyzed with fear, and while the marble roof of the library was wide-open space, the widow's walk itself was only about two feet wide. My back was already against the railing on the edge.

Retreat was impossible.

Casting my eyes about desperately, I saw the small pile of polished stones I had noticed earlier. I picked up a handful and hurled them at the ghostly figure, seemingly without effect. But then I heard a loud banging on the door leading onto the roof, and Ellen yelled out, "Sandy! Sandy! Are you out there? Unlock this door! This is a terrible fire hazard!"

That was when I remembered that while the library itself was sound-proofed, the roof was not.

"Help! Help!" I screamed as loudly as possible, the sound of my voice carrying out over the water.

The figure with the knife seemed to disappear into thin air. I ran to the door, fumbling with the handle until, miraculously, it opened.

"Did you see it?" I yelled. "The ghost! Not a ghost! Someone dressed up like a ghost. She had a knife!"

"A ghost! What are you talking about?"

I grabbed her arm. "Is there another staircase leading out of here?"

"Yes. There's an outside staircase. We needed it for the fire code." She pointed off into the distance across the roof, in the direction the "ghost" had disappeared.

"I think someone just tried to kill me. How did you know I was up here?"

"It was such a beautiful day that I wanted to eat lunch with you outside on the bench. Letitia Rose told me where you were."

"Letitia Rose was too scared to come up here. I'm just glad *you* had the courage."

Ellen patted my arm and slowly managed to loosen my grip on hers. "Letitia Rose isn't scared—at least not during the day. She just prefers to give this place a wide berth. It's not an area associated with celebrations. I come up here almost every day to chase the Mexican kids. They don't have widows walks where they come from. They have their own ghosts around Halloween, but they don't worry about ours. "

She picked up a couple of cigarette butts from the walk and put them into a plastic bag.

"The kids come up here to smoke weed and cigarettes. Other drugs too. I've found needles up here. Condoms. The wind sweeps a lot of this stuff off into the bay, but I come up here regularly to check things out."

"That phony ghost was no Mexican kid. Someone just tried to murder me. We need to call the sheriff."

"You're going to tell the sheriff that your life was threatened by a ghost? Why would anyone want to murder you?" Ellen took my hand. "I have known you for a long time, Sandy. You're a very good person, but you have an extremely lively imagination. You still dream about your blue baby."

"She was blue! Maybe not blue like the bay or the sky but blue all the same."

"Well maybe you just fell asleep up here in the sun and you dreamed about the ghost. Do you have any proof?"

I thought for a minute. There might be fingerprints on the door. But then I remembered my ghostly assailant was wearing black gloves.

I picked up the plastic cup with the remains of my blueberries and strawberries and the napkins I had brought. Then I saw my iPhone laying on the weathered boards by my feet. I had forgotten all about it. I might have been able to take a photo of the ghost—if ghosts come out in photos.

Since my best friend, Ellen, didn't take my ghost story seriously, I didn't think I'd make any headway with the sheriff. Just the thought of meeting with him again made my head throb. I followed Ellen down the stairs to the main floor, where we both worked and seated myself behind the desk.

***

Ellen slipped out from behind the desk without saying goodnight. Letitia Rose left early. By 5:15 the entire first floor was empty.

It was then that the events of the day started to close in on me.

Was it possible I had dreamed up the entire encounter on the roof? I didn't think so. That whole superstition about the widow's walk was ridiculous, anyway. The library had only been built five years earlier, and the whaling industry on the East End had been gone for more than 200 years. There were no sailor's widows walking around up there now. Nevertheless, it would probably be best not to discuss this ghost story with anyone else. It was a mystery I would have to figure out for myself.

And then there were the questions about Messi, about the mysterious drowning of his girlfriend.

I'd promised myself not to stay alone after hours in the library again, but it was the only time I could have some quiet in which to meditate upon, and maybe even solve, the problems plaguing me. Whatever else he was, at least Messi wasn't else a ghost.

I went to the shelves and found a copy of *An American Tragedy*. I flipped through it until I found the drowning scene.

The protagonist has impregnated his girlfriend, a penniless shop girl. Abortions are illegal and considered immoral. Her choices are marriage or disappearing for a while, birthing the baby in secret, then giving it up.

The protagonist has no money either. It would be a struggle, any way you look at it for him to marry the girl and support her. Not only that, but he no longer has any affection for her. Only ambition fills his heart. He has a chance to marry rich. So, he decides to take the pregnant girl for a boat ride, knowing she can't swim. His plan: to push her overboard.

But having been raised in a religious household, his mind is conflicted. And then an accident occurs, the rowboat capsizes and they both fall overboard. She struggles in the water. Screams. He turns his back on her and swims to shore. She drowns.

Has he killed her? He isn't quite sure.

I closed the book. It was quite clear to me that if you allowed a person to drown right in front of you and did not try to rescue them, you were responsible for their death.

You had murdered that person as surely as if you had pushed her head under the water and kept it there.

What had happened to Messi's girlfriend out there on the sea that stormy night?

She must have known how to swim. You couldn't grow up in Pilgrim's Landing without learning how to swim. Even in Brooklyn, you couldn't graduate high school if you weren't able to swim the length of the pool at the local YMCA.

Once more, I pictured Messi as I saw him in the photo featured two years ago on the front page of the *Pilgrim's Landing Star*. His chest bare, his long hair pulled back in a ponytail, his large hands gripping the wheel of his fishing boat.

Was he Neptune or Satan?

I looked up at the rafters of the library. There were no answers hovering there. No clap of thunder or flash of lightning to tell me which vision of Messi was the most correct.

I put the book back on the shelf.

Messi! I needed to check my romantic fantasies. He might have already turned his attention elsewhere. He hadn't acknowledged my waving to him at The Olde Church, and he hadn't contacted me since.

Still, I couldn't stop thinking about him, hoping he'd pay me an after-hours visit while I sat there at the desk. The aura of danger only made the thought more exciting.

Just as I was thinking this, I heard the sound of a brush sweeping along the floor and the metallic noise of a bucket being moved. In the dim light near the stairway, I saw a shadow pushing a large trash can.

I had forgotten that the janitor, Pepe, worked late cleaning up. It was his mop and bucket I almost tripped over when I'd discovered Eddie's body on the ground floor.

"Pepe?"

No answer. The shadow was gone. Had he gone to the men's room? I walked towards the trash can and peered inside.

I saw a pair of shoes sticking out from a pile of paper.

The paper was glistening wet and red.

And the shoes were attached to feet.

I screamed, grabbing the side of the garbage can for balance as I felt my legs wobble beneath my body. My fingers slid over the slick wet blood, and I fell to the floor.

Wiping my hand on my trousers, I crawled back to the desk and picked up the phone to call the sheriff.

Chapter Six

*"No man, for any considerable period, can wear one face to himself
and another to the multitude, without finally getting bewildered
as to which may be the true."*

—Nathaniel Hawthorne, *The Scarlet Letter*

There would be no memorial service at The Olde Church for Pepe. And if the sheriff had dispensed quickly with Eddie's body, I was sure this guy would vanish right before my eyes. I shivered. Someone had tried to kill me on the widow's walk. Now someone had just left a bloody corpse next to my desk. It was unbelievable—and terrifying.

The sensible thing would have been to pack my bags and leave town in the middle of the night. But what about everyone else? Some lunatic serial killer was roaming the library. I wasn't the kind to desert a sinking ship. On the other hand, I wasn't a hero.

Then I thought of someone who was.

My hands were shaking so badly it was hard to push the buttons on my phone, but I managed to call Job at the Mohican's Bar. If he was there, I figured he'd be able to roll his wheelchair back up the street to the library faster than the Sheriff could roll down the window of his car.

And I was right! A huge wave of relief washed over me as Job rolled up the ramp right into the front room of the library. He didn't even blanch when he saw the two legs sticking out from the top of the refuse can. He'd had experience with dead bodies.

He peered into the can, grabbed a pointer used for presentations off the desk and poked around. When he withdrew the stick, the point was red. He took some photos with his iPhone.

When Bill Bronson arrived, he just nodded to Job— took a couple of photos with his own iPhone and motioned for his deputy to grab hold of the guy's legs and pull him out.

Job handed him the pointer. "No hurry getting him out, Bill. He's dead as a doornail. Better wait till the coroner arrives, don't you think?

The sheriff adjusted his cap; the pilgrim lady embroidered on the front seemed to shiver.

"It's real late now, Job, and I happen to know that coroner and Mrs. Symons go to sleep early. Why disturb everyone? As you say, dead is dead. He sure ain't goin' any place, 'cept the morgue, and we can handle that."

He turned towards me: "Miss Nutbaum, you discovered the body? Again? You haven't even signed the first statement, and now we need to draft a second one? And what were *you* doin' here this time of night, Job—making friends with the pretty lady?"

Job rolled up so close to him I thought he was going to run him over. "Not all of us are lucky enough to have a gal in every port," Job said. Then he took out a handkerchief and spit in it.

"Well, now, Job, I'd be careful if I was you. Never know when she might chop you up for—what's that stuff they eat—matzos?"

Job winced. "As I seem to remember, Bill, Harvey Shapiro on the town Board helps pay your salary, so I'd be careful how you talk. As for Symons, I suggest you call him before all that blood coagulates and no one can tell the time of death."

The sheriff made a couple of calls. Job rolled over to one of the oak reading tables and motioned for me to follow him. He did not disappoint in the cool and calm department, and I found my heartbeat beginning to return to normal just by being close to him. Symons, the coroner, arrived shortly, along with two tall men carrying a body bag.

"Hi Jake," Job nodded to one, "how's little John?"

Jake tipped his hat. "Good. Growing fast. Thanks for asking."

"Glad to see you, Symons. Bill here says you go to bed early. Maybe you need your hours reduced or something. What do you say?"

Symons bent over the body and then straightened up. "Don't listen to any rumors like that, Job. The missus may be under the weather from time to time but I'm just fine."

We heard a heavy step on the stairs leading up from the ground floor level. The sheriff pulled out a gun.

I ran behind the desk and picked up a scissors.

We all stared at the staircase and then Winston appeared before us.

Winston, usually impeccably dressed in his white shirt, vest and polished boots, looked disheveled and confused. His cap, filled with 4-H pins and other strange insignias, was turned round, and his grey hair was snarled and uncombed.

"What's going on here? I...kind of fell asleep down there...and all of a sudden I heard all this noise, and...." He seemed to have finally noticed the two legs sticking out of the trash can.

"Jesus!" Winston's pale face seemed to get even paler, his knees started to buckle. The sheriff managed to catch him before he hit the ground, settling him in a chair.

"Hey, Miss Librarian, can you get this man some water?"

There was a cooler in plain sight, but it was obvious to me that a man like the sheriff preferred issuing orders.

I brought Winston a cup of cool water, then excused myself and went to the lady's room to wash the blood off my hands.

Winston looked a wreck. I wondered if maybe we should call an ambulance or something, but the sheriff had other plans.

He leaned over him. "Now, Winston. Did you hear or see anything unusual? What time, do you...think...you fell asleep?"

Winston gulped down the water. "I can't say. I was looking at the most interesting document, and my eyes are not as good as they once were, and I turned on the special light I have down there, and then I used my magnifier, but the ink had faded so... I suppose I must have had one of my small catnaps or something. Then I heard all kinds of stomping noises up here and came up to investigate."

I felt suddenly exhausted. I sank down into a chair at the reading table.

Job wheeled himself over to my side and took my arm. He turned to the sheriff.

"Well, then. I guess this situation is in good hands. I'll say good night now. I think the lady could use a drink."

The sheriff turned to me. "I'm happy to let her go in your custody, Job. And you, Miss Librarian, do not plan to leave town until after I have obtained your statements."

I nodded and followed Job out the library door and down the ramp to the street.

"Thanks, Job," I said, as we walked and rolled back up the street to Mohican's. "That sheriff is a piece of work."

"Yeah. Bad work. He'll leave you alone once he sees you have some friends. Can't say if Messi is an asset in that department or not."

"The sheriff doesn't like Messi?"

Job laughed. "That would be an understatement. "

That had been my gut feeling—and the confrontation at the memorial service had seemed to confirm that. Still, I wondered what was behind it.

Job rolled ahead of me into the bar and found us a table.

I ordered a Guinness, Job a scotch.

"What's the story with them? With him and Messi?"

He ignored my question, raising his glass.

"To your health," he said, touching his glass to mine. "As for anything concerning Messi—you'll have to ask him."

I would have loved to have asked Messi a lot of things. Easier said than done.

"Winston seemed pretty upset. He's very old-fashioned and formal, but I like him. How old do you think he is?"

Job looked up at the ceiling, as if searching for an answer.

"Winston was always old. One of those descendants of the pilgrims who carries his pedigree around with him for everyone to see. On the town council, of course, trustee of the library. Lives off what is left of the family money—probably not much. Drinks more than he should. But then, people would say I do, too."

"The library is lucky to have you so involved. You're a great role model for the kids."

"Just about everyone in town is involved with the library in one way or another. It's a great source of pride. Bigger than the one in Bliss Bay. More marble per square foot than a mausoleum. I'm on the town board and that makes me a trustee of the library, like it or not—but I've always liked kids, and since I'm not likely to have any of my own, I figured teaching art to the kids would be one way of leaving a legacy."

I could understand that. My only try for kids ended badly—my baby girl dead on arrival. That had been five years ago. It still kept me up on many dark nights. The doctor had warned me not to look at her, but I hadn't listened. She was perfect. Except she was blue.

"You have such an expressive face," Job said. "I love your hair. Where did that white streak come from?

"My dad. People on the street used to ask him which barber had done it, but it was entirely natural. So is mine."

Job continued to stare at me. I was beginning to feel a little uncomfortable.

"I'd very much like to paint you. Do you think Messi would mind?"

This really threw me for a loop. Was Job coming on to me? And why did everyone in town assume Messi and I were a couple? Just because Job was in a wheelchair didn't mean he had no feelings or urges. I wondered if he could he perform sexually.

"It's very flattering of you to ask, Job. Messi certainly has no claims on me, so that's not the issue. The thing is, I'm still new in town, and I don't feel comfortable drawing more attention to myself than I already have. It's.... It's too soon."

"Too soon to make a commitment to Pilgrim's Landing, or too soon to make a promise to me?"

"Both," I said. "Too soon for decisions of any kind. Besides, we both need to work tomorrow."

I took one more long swallow of my beer, said goodnight, thanked him, and made my way back out into the warm summer night.

***

I was still a little wobbly when I got home. Even though it was only a little after nine, all I wanted to do was roll into bed and forget about my day. I took off my black trousers and white shirt—my librarian's uniform—and threw them into my laundry basket. Then I put on one of my old baggy T-shirts, this one featuring a fire engine and the words, "Our Heroes, 911."

Too tired even to wash my face, I climbed into bed and pulled the covers up to my ears.

There was a knock on my door.

Ellen. Looking for a little comfort?

To my surprise, it was Messi.

I hoped the fact that my house was pitch dark would hide my imperfections as a housekeeper. I invited him inside.

He plunked himself down at the kitchen table as if it were his own home.

"This dump looks just like it did when Old Man Jensen lived here. Guess you're not big on decorating."

I opened the refrigerator and took out a cold beer, glad I'd had the foresight to stock some Guinness.

"Be right back," I told him, and I ran into the bedroom to find my vintage kimono. I ran my hands through my hair, trying to fluff it out a little so I looked less like a wet sheep dog.

Messi cleared his throat, alerting me to his presence, having apparently followed me into the bedroom. He turned his back while I slipped into the robe.

"Don't get dressed up for me. If anything—get undressed. Into a bathing suit. I thought you might appreciate a little night fishing."

I might indeed—and most anything else Messi was pleased to offer—but tonight was not an ordinary night.

"So, you haven't heard."

"What haven't I heard? I've been out on the boat all day, gutting fish."

"There's been another murder. The janitor. I think it was Pepe, but it could have been another janitor. There are a couple who work different shifts."

Messi pursed his lips, as if he had just tasted something very sour.

"A janitor? Why would anyone murder a janitor?"

"I agree. It doesn't make any sense."

Messi took my hand. "And *you* found him?"

I nodded.

"There have always been lots of accidental deaths out here—car accidents, drownings, someone run over by a tractor, drug overdoses. But murder? Not really our style. It must have been terrifying for you—for him. Was there a lot of blood? Get me his full name. I know a couple of Hispanic families who work round here. Someone should pay them some mind."

Messi stood and pulled me up next to him. "In the meantime, the way I look at it, all this is more reason you need some restorative activity. Can you swim?"

"Of course, I can swim. I learned to dive through the waves at my aunt's house in Rockaway Beach. The water is so rough there, it attracts surfers from all over Brooklyn."

Messi smiled. "Let's do it," he said. "Get yourself into a bathing suit—or—of course—if you prefer to swim nude, I can deal with that too. But take along a sweatshirt and jeans, too. It can get cold out on the water."

I grabbed my bathing suit, made a quick change—didn't know if Messi was peeking—hoped he was—my hair might be getting gray, but my body was still good. Pulled on a sweatshirt and jeans and let Messi lead me down the road to the shore below. There was a rubber dingy nosed onto the sand. He lifted me inside, grabbed a paddle and pushed us off, gliding out into the bay.

For the first time all evening, I realized what a glorious evening it was. There was a full moon, and the sky was a deep purple. The water was surprisingly rough—the white caps now and again sending a spray of water in my face. I found a blanket in the dingy and wrapped it around my shoulders.

I could see lights along the shoreline, but I wasn't quite sure which direction we were going and I didn't care. Eventually, Messi pulled up to a small fishing boat. He tied the dingy up to the back of it and climbed quickly aboard.

He turned and extended a hand. "Bring the blanket and hold on tight," he said, swinging me up out of the dingy onto the deck of the boat as if I weighed no more than a feather. "Sit," he said, pointing to a large cushion on a benchlike seat.

"'Fraid it's a mite too chilly and rough for a good swim, but the fish love weather like this."

He looked over the side, down at the water. "Could be there are still some stripers around. Have you ever gone fishing?"

"Once or twice when I was a kid. My father took me to Sheepshead Bay. We sat on the dock with a couple of fishing rods. It was boring."

"Boring!" Messi's turquoise eyes flashed.

He pulled me to a standing position. "I've been fishing since I was three-years-old and I have never, not even for a minute, ever been bored." He glared at me. "There are lots of people who bore me—but fish? Never!"

I decided not to take this exchange personally.

There were a couple of rods, stuck in tubular harnesses, and Messi carefully lifted one of them out. He took out a can of something that smelled very fishy from a wooden box built into the stern of the boat. I saw that the bucket was full of tiny shimmering silver fish. He grabbed a couple with a sun-darkened muscular hand and threaded them onto the barbed hook dangling from the rod. He repeated this with the other rod.

"Silver minnows. Sometimes I use bunker. They sell phony ones—lures, they call them—but I don't think there is really any substitute for live bait."

During this disgusting activity, I did my best to look interested. He handed me one of the rods, threw the line overboard and put his arms around me, letting out the line.

"So, what do you think we'll catch?"

"Probably porgies, maybe fluke."

He looked out over the water as the boat bobbed up and down. The moonlight cast little diamonds of light on the tips of the wavelets.

"'It's the very error of the moon: She comes more nearer earth than she was wont, and makes men mad.' That's Shakespeare."

"And women? I thought poets used the moon as a symbol of inconstancy."

"I think you know the wrong women."

Messi's strong arms held me closer.

"How do you know which fish are running?"

"How do you know it's spring? You smell the flowers—I smell the sea! I see the birds! Yes—I see the moon. I feel the wind—I feel the temperature of the sea. Some fish like to bathe in the moonlight—others hide in the deep. And the pure beauty of it! If you ever saw a marlin—iridescent blue like a sapphire—break the surface of the water leaping into the sky, like some magical creature half-bird, half-fish—and then cut down again in a perfect arc, like a dancer— amazing!"

I held tight to the fishing rod. There was a lot to learn. "You say you love the fish, but you kill them. You make your living killing fish!"

"I don't always kill them. Once or twice they almost killed me. A tuna pulled me overboard. And the sharks—I'd rather not even discuss those guys. Fishing is more than a sport, it's part of the circle of life. I kill them so someone else, or even another fish, can live. That's one of the reasons you need to learn to eat a clam. The only real sin in life is to kill a fish with no intention of eating it."

If Messi was going to show off his knowledge of the sea, I had to show off my knowledge of books.

"'For whatever we lose (like a you or a me),

It's always our self we find in the sea.'

"That's e.e. cummings."

Messi laughed. "Was he a fisherman?"

I figured if he wrote about the sea, he probably caught a few fish from time to time, so I lied. "Yes, of course."

I was just beginning to really enjoy the feel of those strong, warm arms around me when there was a tug on the end of the line.

"Oh my God! I think I caught something!"

Messi tightened his grip on the rod. "Not so fast. This is just the beginning. Let out the line! Faster! Faster—or the rod will snap in half!"

He took hold of the rod, and he pulled me over to the far end of the boat. Then he pulled me back and, holding the rod and my arm with one hand, started the boat's motor. Now we were riding high on the choppy water and the spray was hitting me full in the face!

"We got to run with the fish! Tire him out! Look over there!"

Messi pointed straight ahead and there, splashing for all it was worth, was a very large, shape, with silvery scales that caught the moonlight like a streak of star dust.

"I think you hooked a striper! They're usually gone by this time! Good job!"

He cut the motor, started up some other machinery (an anchor?), and bent over the edge of the boat, grabbing the line in his hands and pulling. I held on to the rod with all my strength. Suddenly, there, alongside the boat, was a huge fish with a gaping mouth. Messi hoisted him out of the water with something that looked like a huge butterfly net.

The thing was almost as big as I was! It lay there twitching in the net until Messi lifted it up and laid it on the deck at my feet, still squirming, gills flapping. He took the rod out of my hands, somehow detached the hook from its mouth and put the rod back in its holder.

I started jumping up and down like a kid, yelling, "I caught a giant fish! I caught a giant fish!"

Messi whipped out a camera from somewhere and began clicking away while I knelt by the flopping fish and smiled.

"I'll clean and filet it, and you and Ellen can eat it all summer!"

I shook my head. The sight of the now nearly lifeless thing, whose scales had already lost the quick-silver shine of the sea, would have been enough to turn me off even if I liked fish. I'd had enough of death.

"You really won't eat it? "

"If I brought you a half a cow and said you could feed on it all summer, what would you say?"

"All that red blood is a little off-putting, but if I were hungry enough, I would eat it."

"I'm not hungry enough."

And the truth was, Messi had caught the fish. I just held on to the rod. At this point, I was cold, clothes soaked, shivering. The terrors of the day had abated with Messi's strong arms around me, but suddenly they hit me with a vengeance, and I wandered back to the cushioned seat in the rear of the boat and pulled the blanket around me.

Messi cut the motor. The boat bucked up and down on the waves. He bent over me, reached into some crevice on the side of the pad I was lying on, pulled out another blanket and gently wrapped it around me.

It was pretty dark, despite the moon and stars so I didn't get a good look at the boat, but I knew it was big enough to have a cabin below deck—a kitchen, bathroom, a place to sleep, a place to escape the cold and the waves.

But I said nothing. I had the distinct feeling that he was not yet ready to reveal any more about himself. If I asked to go inside, he would say "It's too soon."

"I'm sorry it was so cold out here for you tonight. But at least you didn't get seasick."

"Nope. I don't get seasick, but the rocking of the boat makes me a little dizzy, and very sleepy."

Messi kissed the top of my head—the only body part not covered by the blanket.

"Hang in there, Miss Librarian. I'll have you back on shore in about 10 minutes."

I hadn't even closed my eyes when I saw a lot of splashing a few yards from shore and before I could even rise from the pad I was lying on, Messi was knee deep in the water, handing a rope to a skinny kid with long black hair who looked vaguely familiar.

The kid quickly busied himself tying the boat up while Messi scrambled back aboard and gently pulled me to a sitting position.

"This pretty lady caught a striper," he said. "Throw some ice over it and we can divvy it up tomorrow." Messi helped me climb down a small ladder into the water.

"Say hello to the new librarian, Hawkeye. Miss Nussbaum."

Hawkeye nodded.

"We met the other day," I said. "You take pictures for the *Pilgrim's Landing Star*, right?"

Hawkeye nodded shyly again. I seemed to have this effect on some people. They were scared to talk to me.

"Good to see you, Hawkeye. Hope to see you again in the library. We have a bunch of books, including *Moby Dick*, that I really think you'll enjoy."

This speech seemed to scare him even more and he turned away and fumbled with the rope.

"Hawkeye has a number of talents, among them being a super fisherman. Come on," he took my hand, "we're going home." Messi pointed to a light, directly above us on a low cliff.

The sandy road to the cottage was steep but easy to navigate in the moonlight, the sand cool and deep beneath our bare toes. Messi held my hand the whole way.

When we arrived, he pushed open the door and motioned for me to take a seat at the kitchen table.

While I sat there, Messi went into another room and came back with a large t-shirt that said *Sands End* and featured a tall white lighthouse against a turquoise sea.

"I'll take you home whenever you want, but I think you need to warm up a little first."

He pointed me toward his bedroom. The double bed was made so tight it looked like you could bounce a quarter off it. Next to the bed was a small night table with a drawer. The space was immaculate, the walls, ceiling and floor all whitewashed. A plaid shirt and a couple of pair of jeans hung on pegs in the wall. In one corner was a small chest that looked like something captured from a pirate ship.

I peeled off my bathing suit and put on the t-shirt, which smelled of bleach and came down to my knees. Still shivering, I wrapped myself back up in the blanket. One thing was sure. Messi was a better housekeeper than I was. But this was more than neatness—there was something sterile, impersonal about his place. More like a Monk's cell than a home.

There was a knock on the bedroom door.

"Safe to come in?"

"It's your house."

He came in and sat on the bed next to me.

"This room," I said. "It's so bare. Almost as if nobody lived here."

"I'm away for long periods of time. I go to Key West for the winter. I don't like to leave a large footprint behind."

A footprint or evidence of activities he would rather not share with others? What was it Hal had said? Some people thought Messi's boat carried more than fish and tourists.

"There are no photos—of family or friends—not even a photo of you catching a giant tuna!"

Messi laughed. "There are plenty of them in the *Pilgrim's Landing Star*! I don't like to keep photos. They're so...so dead. A pinpoint in time. Like a butterfly captured and pinned down in one of those glass cases. I prefer real life."

I pointed to the scarred and dented metal chest on the floor near the door.

"What's in there?" Messi opened the chest. Inside was a knapsack. "I keep this bag handy for stormy weather."

He pulled out a wet suit, a pair of rubber boots, flippers, a canteen of water, a package of high-energy bars, a couple of flares, and a small metal box of matches.

"Sometimes at sea there are emergencies. I like to be prepared."

He zipped up the bag and put it back in the chest.

And then he gently unwrapped the blanket and drew me towards him. He moved his fingers over my face, and then he kissed me.

That was when I gave up any thought of going home.

He pulled back the covers of the bed and lifted off the t-shirt he had lent me.

"You know that Bob Dylan song? 'Lay, Lady Lay?' Whatever colors you have in your mind, I will show them to you and make them shine."

"Show me."

And then he did.

Afterwards, he reached over from the bed and opened the drawer of the night table, extracting a baggy filled with marijuana. He took a big pinch and used it to roll a joint. He sealed the finished product by sticking it in his mouth and withdrawing it through pressed lips, then he ran a lit match under it, lighting it, taking a hit, and offering it to me as he exhaled a cloud of smoke. I shook my head.

***

Sometime in the middle of the night, I woke up. I had refused Messi's offer of a reefer. Vodka was more my style, but even so I felt woozy and a little confused. Where the hell was I?

The room was pitch black and as my head began to clear, I reached over to Messi's side of the bed.

Empty.

I tried to remember where the bathroom was. Fortunately, the space was small and there were only a couple of doors. I was naked, my soggy sweatshirt, jeans and bathing suit somewhere on the floor. I'd left my flip-flops in the boat. What had I done?

I felt around on the floor until I located my bathing suit, which of course was still soaking wet. I had no idea where Messi went or when he would return. I was about to grab one of his shirts and a pair of his pants, with the idea of hitching a ride from some kind soul, when I caught sight of a bunch of twinkling lights from the window.

I pulled open the curtain and looked down the cliff to the water. The pinpoints of light came from directly below me. Noise travels easily across water, and I could hear splashing sounds and muffled voices though nothing distinct enough to make out.

I thought of taking the path back down the cliff to see more clearly what was going on—and maybe to find someone to bring me home—but I had no flashlight, and the moon, which had been so bright just hours ago, now was shrouded by a dark cloud.

I was still looking out the window when Messi came in through the door.

He turned my head for a kiss, but I suppose my scowl dissuaded him.

"Hi! Forgot to tell you that I get started really early in the morning on my fishing rounds. Made you a cup of coffee. And brought back your shoes."

He set the coffee down on the night table. He placed my flip-flops on the side of the bed.

I pointed to the pin pricks of light and the splashing below. "Do all those fishermen work for you?"

"Some do, and some don't."

"What do you catch?"

"Depends on the weather."

"Are they digging for clams?"

"Sometimes."

He pulled a shirt off its hook and then fumbled around in the pirate chest until he came up with a pair of men's shorts. He knotted a piece of rope and put it through the loops.

"Slip into these and I'll get you home before the sun comes up."

The coffee was warm and helped clear my head. Clear enough to know there was something fishy going on here even if I couldn't quite figure out what.

Messi was a commercial fisherman. Third generation. He fished for tuna that Japanese agents flew across to Japan in great containers called coffins. He fished for bass, bluefish, and fluke. He took sportsmen way out in the ocean to fish for marlin, to see dolphins and humpback whales.

None of these fish were caught in knee-deep water in the middle of the night. People who dug for clams could do it more easily during the day.

He put my bathing suit, and the rest of my soggy clothes in a plastic bag, which he handed to me.

"You look kind of sexy in men's clothes."

"Maybe you should keep some women's stuff around. Might come in handy for your women guests."

Messi stopped in the kitchen where there was now a bowl full of clams. He picked one up—took a large pocketknife from his pocket—and in an instant had opened the shell.

He held up the clam.

"I'll give you $100 to eat this clam. "

I shook my head. "That's a mighty sharp knife."

Messi closed it against his thigh and put it in his pocket. "Belonged to my father and his father before him. I can gut a 25-pound striper with this knife in under three minutes."

Messi opened the front door and led me down a short, narrow road where his old VW was parked. He paused by the car door. "I haven't had a woman guest for a long time." He opened the door. "Especially one who doesn't eat seafood."

There was an official looking letter stuck under the windshield.

Messi pulled it out, ripped it open and tossed it into the glove compartment. "What is it?"

"Just a note from our friendly sheriff. An application for a commercial fishing license."

"But you told me you and your family have been fishing these waters since the 1920s."

Messi put the car in gear. "Commercial fishing licenses are handed down from generation to generation like so many things on the East End. It's very difficult to get a new license because you need to have hundreds of hours at sea working on a licensed boat in order to qualify. I get this stupid letter every year, just some friendly harassment from the sheriff to remind me who's in charge."

"And you put up with that?"

"I pick my fights, and right now I'd rather enjoy the good things that are happening"

He took his hand off the wheel and placed it on my thigh.

"This is a town where all the parking spaces in town are marked with white lines. Any car whose back fender is over the line, gets a fifty dollar fine. I am not a guy who likes to park in between lines, but I'd rather pay the ticket than spend all my time in court."

There was something wrong with this explanation, complimentary as it was. Messi didn't seem like a man to ignore a provocation. I thought again of the splashing below his bungalow.

"Do you catch lobster?"

"Nope. Doesn't really feel sporting to me. Dropping a bunch of boxes and then waiting till some unsuspecting creature wanders in. I'd rather dangle some bait and see what comes along. Play with the reel and rod and give the fish a fighting chance. "

"Do you ever cut them loose?"

"Depends on how hungry I am. "

We drove the rest of the way to my house in silence. Messi knew I didn't buy his fishing story or his sheriff story, but the sun was just coming up and the sky had turned pink; it was too beautiful a morning to argue about anything.

I wanted to believe that Messi was better than he probably was. I also hoped he was too hungry to set me loose.

***

Notes from Sandra, Assistant Librarian
Clam: Arctica Islandica
Class: Bivalvia
Phylum: Mollusa

Taste: Probably slimy, rubbery, to be eaten only in an emergency

Chapter Seven

"Perhaps I should not have been a fisherman, he thought. But that was the thing that I was born for."

—Ernest Hemingway, *The Old Man and the Sea*

I slept late the next day, catching up on lost sleep. Again, I dreamed of the blue baby, and I woke up gasping. It was bad enough to prompt me to call in sick.

"You get some rest, girl. Letitia Rose said. "You been dealing with some *stuff*. Anyway, I'm closing the library this afternoon in recognition of Pepe. A good man. Even if he was one of those Mexicans who probably swam here, he was one of ours."

Good old Letitia Rose. She would honor "doing the right thing" over her own prejudices.

As for me—I slept for half the day, and when I woke up, felt not the slightest bit better about anything that had happened recently.

I was annoyed at myself for falling hook, line, and sinker, for Messi, who was probably a smuggler and possibly something much worse.

I kept picturing Pepe's legs sticking out of that refuse can. All he wanted was a better life. I opened my purse and took out the little silver cross he had given me. It had protected me up on the widow's walk, but it hadn't protected him.

Who would murder a janitor? He had nothing to steal. He didn't bother anyone. Didn't come on duty until evening, after the library was closed.

And then I remembered. How I had almost tripped over his can and mop the night Eddie was murdered. How I had met him after I sneaked into Eddie's office to investigate on my own.

Pepe was murdered because he had seen something he wasn't meant to see! The phony ghost who tried to murder me on the roof? Maybe I was a target for the same reason—fear that I'd seen something I wasn't supposed to see.

Of course! That seemed clear to me now. But if that was true, it also meant that I was indirectly responsible for Pepe's death!

I tried to remember now how many people I'd told that I had almost tripped over his mop and bucket. I knew that I had told the sheriff. I knew that I had told Job. I think I had even mentioned it to Ellen and Letitia Rose!

I flopped back onto my bed. Someone who was a regular in the library was a murderer—that seemed clear. Of course, it was also possible that the people I had told could have mentioned it to others. There was Hal, the editor of the *Pilgrim Star*. There was Hawkeye. It could be either of them, and others, too. One thing was beginning to be clear to me: something illegal was going on in the library, right under the nose of Miss Correctness herself—and either she was in denial about it or she was up to her neck in it.

By this time, it was about four in the afternoon, and I was beginning to get hungry. I found a can of tuna in the refrigerator and made myself a sandwich.

It wasn't true that I didn't like fish. I just didn't like fresh fish. Canned was okay. Even an occasional fried flounder was acceptable.

I was eating my tuna sandwich quite happily when I heard a knocking at the door, and a familiar voice called out "Hi, Sandy. It's me. Ellen."

She wasn't hysterical and needy this time. On the contrary, dressed in black trousers and over-sized no-iron white shirt, she was ready for business.

She gave me a pat on the back and looked me up and down. "I figured you could use a hug today, so I came over."

I guess she figured that "use a hug" was just an expression because she didn't actually put her arms around me. In truth, Ellen was not the hugging kind. In place of a hug, she pulled out one of the kitchen chairs and sat down.

"Letitia Rose is worried about you, too," she said. "She gave me strict orders to stay with you until dinnertime to be sure you were getting proper nourishment. She has you pegged as the stiff-upper-lip type of person who needs extra attention because you'll never ask for it yourself. "

"Good old Letitia Rose! It takes one to know one," I said. I could have added that Ellen to the list, too.

"Holy spirits above! Are you eating canned tuna? And with a fisherman for a boyfriend? What are you thinking?"

"Who said Messi was my boyfriend?"

"Heard he took you out last night for some... night fishing. Looks like the night air did you a world of good!"

"Yes and no. He's still a mystery to me. All I really know about him is he is a very good fisherman—and seems to have a way with the ladies. But it looks as if the whole town has an obsession with Messi. Where he goes, who he's with, what he has done or hasn't done. What's that all about?"

"Most of the people in town believe he has supernatural powers. They say he can breathe underwater. Did you know he was found floating far out in the ocean four days after his boat capsized—hanging on to a pair of rubber boots that he claims held him up all that time?"

I almost choked on that piece of news. "He was floating in the Atlantic Ocean for four days? What about sharks!"

"Supernatural powers! I'm telling you. It might be better if you found someone who could walk on top of the water, like Moses, but I know for a fact, Messi isn't Jewish."

"I think if he submits to any God, it's Neptune."

For the first time I wondered if Messi was attracted to me *because* I was Jewish and, like him, an outsider. Was I an exotic catch? And what about my attraction to him? A working-class Italian fisherman and possible murderer? Not the best pick for a respectable middle-class woman like me.

One thing was sure. When it came to love and attraction, it was a waste of energy to try and figure it out. Even if you could, it still probably wouldn't make any sense.

***

The next day was business as usual at Pilgrim's Landing library. *The Star* lay in front of the door. It did not have any photos on the front page. In the back, under "classified ads" was a small notice in Spanish, under the heading "Vaya Con Dios." It stated simply the dates of Pepe's birth and death, and it was signed "Maria Gonzalez."

I didn't know if Maria was his wife, daughter, or sister. There was no address.

Letitia Rose told me she'd sent flowers "from the staff of Pilgrim's Landing library," but I wanted to send something personal. I had a vague idea of returning the little silver cross to his remaining family, but I couldn't help but think that it had protected me so far from "The Library Murderer." I was afraid to lose that protection—so I put it back in my purse.

There was no line of curiosity-seekers outside the library. Only Sally Brier Montgomery, the woman who had shrieked and fallen down at Eddie's memorial. She was a regular at the library and seemed a special friend of Letitia Rose. Her specialty was reading the library copy of *The New York Times* every day and tearing out the recipes. Why one of those three-name pilgrim people couldn't buy her own copy of the New York Times was beyond me, but, as Ellen explained, "Sally's husband died a year ago. She comes to the library for company."

"Good morning, Miss Nussbaum," she greeted me. "Lovely day today."

Indeed, it was a lovely day. The seagulls swooped and called; the clouds were small white puffs of cotton against a deep blue sky.

Sally Brier Montgomery did not know that Pepe had been murdered a couple of nights ago. And, if she did know, I didn't think it would cloud her day.

Sally sat down at the oak reading table while I took a seat behind the desk. Ellen wandered in and set up her computer.

"Looks like Cousin Abigail doesn't feel up to coming to the East End to clear out Eddie's house. She used to visit a lot while Eddie and I were growing up—I was fond of her. Treated me like the niece she never had. Asked me to go through the place and take whatever I want. Don't know if I'm up for wandering around the house now. More like a mausoleum than a home. "

I was pretty sure Ellen wouldn't take anything of value for herself—sometimes Pilgrim's Landing "correctness" can go too far. I figured she needed a little help from a more practical friend. Me. Besides, I would love to see how the wealthiest families in Pilgrim's Landing really lived.

"I'll go with you! We'll do it together!"

But before I could say another word, we heard a scream.

The voice was unmistakable—it belonged to Sally Montgomery, and it was coming from the lady's room.

I picked up a pair of scissors from the desk and, with a sinking feeling in my chest, ran with Ellen toward the lady's room. We both pushed on the door, but it seemed to be stuck.

"Sally! Sally! What's happening? Are you all right? Open the door!"

Ellen ran back to the desk and called the sheriff just as Letitia Rose came through the library door.

"It's Sally Montgomery," Ellen yelled. "She's locked herself in the Ladies' room!"

Without missing a beat, Letitia made her way to the bathroom door. "Sally, it's me, Letitia Rose! You open this door right now before Bill Bronson comes with that flat-faced deputy of his and destroys our library. And stop that screaming. Isn't anyone else can hear you, 'cause we are padded for noise-control."

Letitia Rose reached into her large flowered purse and took out a couple of hairpins. She inserted one of them into the lock and motioned for us to push.

The lock sprang open, but it took all three of us pushing to open the door because Sally Montgomery was sitting on the floor in front of it.

She pointed at some object on top of the sink. It had a metallic look, and the sink itself was filled with a red liquid.

"Don't anybody move," yelled Sheriff Bill Bronson as he stormed through the library door with his gun drawn.

"Now, you just put that gun away, Bill Bronson. We do not allow firearms in our library."

Bronson motioned to the squashed nose deputy who cautiously approached the Ladies' room and peered in.

"You might help this lady to her feet young man, before you get that mess in the sink all over my library."

Letitia took one arm, and the deputy took the other, and they led Sally to a seat at the reading table.

"It's so terrible, Lettie. Everything is changed now that Charles is gone. Nothing makes any sense to me anymore," Sally sobbed, clinging to Letitia Rose.

The Sheriff took a few pictures with his iPhone. Then he grabbed a couple of paper towels and retrieved a large pocketknife from the bathroom sink. The knife was covered with what, by now, I assumed was blood. It dripped onto the white marble floor.

"Anyone have a plastic bag?"

Ellen pulled one out from one of the shelves behind the desk.

The sheriff held up the knife as Ellen positioned the bag beneath it.

"Wait!" Letitia Rose said, moving closer to get a better look. "That knife! Let me see that. Just hold it right there!"

She reached into her large purse and felt around. She felt around again. Then she walked over to the oak reading table and spilled a few things out on the table. I saw a pack of gum, a flashlight, a comb, a package of safety pins, an iPad, an iPhone, a bunch of keys, a photo of a young man—and then she scooped it all up and back into her purse and turned to face the sheriff.

"My knife is gone! Someone stole my knife! "

The sheriff dangled the knife in front of Letitia Rose. "Are you telling me this is your knife? Are you aware that this might be a murder weapon?"

Letitia Rose nodded and held tight to the back of the chair.

"I will need your statement."

I had rarely seen Letitia Rose rattled, but she seemed suddenly unsteady on her feet.

I put my arm around her, and she leaned up against me. Then she turned her head to face the sheriff.

"I just gave it to you!"

The sheriff motioned to his deputy, who backed out of the bathroom. He dropped the knife into the plastic bag. He went back into the bathroom and took a sample of the red water in a paper cup and gave it to his deputy.

"You better hire another janitor. It's a real mess in there."

He took some yellow police-tape from out of his pocket that said, "Police Line Do Not Cross," and taped it across the bathroom door.

Then the sheriff looked at me and held out his hand for the keys to the library.

"Ellen—get some crayons and make a sign. Pilgrim's Landing library is closed until further notice."

Letitia Rose, Sally Montgomery and I put our arms around each other and literally held each other up, and then the sheriff ushered us all, one by one, out the door.

***

So, it turned out, I suddenly had some time on my hands with no place to go and nothing to do.

In New York City, that would have been a good thing. Nothing to do in the Big Apple usually meant coffee at the Italian bistro on the corner of Madison Avenue; a leisurely walk down the avenue; a glimpse of the young woman with the blue hair and long dangling earrings, who was walking six, maybe seven dogs of different sizes and breeds (how did she manage to keep them all from attacking each other? Surely there was a lesson to be learned there); it could mean a shopping expedition, stopping at one of the shops along the way to buy a pair of shoes or a pair of earrings. Nothing to do in New York City was plenty to do and provided me enough stimulation and food-for-thought to last for days.

But here in Pilgrim's Landing, nothing to do meant nothing to do. It meant too much time to think and obsess about a dangerous relationship with a man rumored to have supernatural powers; it meant visions of an innocent janitor, whose blood had actually stained my right hand and my trousers; it meant constantly replaying the memory of a strange ghostly figure on the widow's walk of the library and knowing that some lunatic killer was on the loose.

So, I pulled on a pair of shorts, put on my flip-flops, and took a walk down the road that ran from my cottage through a bunch of old birch and pine trees down to the bay, and I tried to put all that bad stuff out of my mind.

It was one of those gorgeous, clear days on the East End, with not a cloud in the sky, the sun shining off the water, creating just enough warmth to make you want to take a swim, but then, as you got closer, occasionally sending up a cool bit of spray to remind you that it was still a little too early for a dip.

I kicked off my shoes and dug my toes into the sand. Then I walked along the shore, the cool water washing over my feet, the tide gently flowing over the smooth, colored stones below, like a glass window into another world.

I waded a little way into the water and scooped up a smooth, yellow rock, and then another—white with a dark vein running through it—like the pile of smooth rocks the Mexican kids had left on the widow's walk. There were shells, too—flimsy yellow shells that I remembered from my days in Rockaway, known as "sailors toenails."

I would pass on the toenails. My immediate association was Messi, whose toes I had not yet carefully examined but imagined to be as perfect as all the rest of his parts.

Down by the edge of the beach, I could see a couple of men digging in the water. Clamming, I imagined. The way it ought to be done, in daylight—not like the strange splashing in the middle of the night below Messi's house.

I filled my pocket with enough smooth stones to give me a satisfying sense of connecting with my new home. Then I sat down on the sand and stared at the water. The gentle sound of it lapping against the shore seemed, at last, to calm my nerves and spirit. I lay back against the sand and listened to the soothing, hypnotic rhythm of it.

At some point, I fell asleep. I don't know for how long. But when I opened my eyes, the sun was high in the sky, and my arms and legs (and no doubt my face) had turned red.

I still had much to learn about Pilgrim's Landing. Today's lesson: sunscreen.

My skin felt tender and hot as I climbed back to my cabin.

I took the key out of my pocket and opened the door.

As soon as I stepped inside, I felt it—that crazy city-bred sense of danger!

I held the door open and peered inside.

I scrounged amongst the pebbles in my pocket until I found the small silver cross Pepe had given me.

Was I just imagining things—or was that box of Kate's cookies in a new position on my kitchen table?

The door to my bedroom was open. I usually left it closed. Had I closed it this morning before I left? I couldn't remember—but I knew I didn't want to go inside that room alone.

Unfortunately, since my nearest neighbor was about a half mile away, I didn't have much choice.

I picked up a wooden breadboard from the kitchen table and walked into the cabin.

"Hello!" I called out.

Silence.

I raised the breadboard over my head and entered the bedroom.

To my relief, no one jumped out. It was empty.

I'd never been much of a housekeeper, as I'd be the first to admit and anyone who knew me would confirm, but I was very careful with certain items that I wanted to be able to locate quickly.

One of these items was a pair of stiletto shoes that I always placed next to my bed, ready to be used in an emergency—be it in love or war. These shoes were not where I'd left them, now stashed at right angles to each other on the floor.

I looked next at the small night table next to my bed. I always placed an extra pair of glasses on top, but someone had pushed the glasses to the edge of the table where they might easily fall off—not a place I'd ever leave them.

Okay. Someone had clearly been inside my cabin—I just hoped to hell they weren't still there.

There were still a couple of places where they could be hiding. The bathroom—whose door was open. Or the closet—whose door was closed.

I walked quietly over to the closet, raised the breadboard over my head, and opened the door.

My clothes had been moved around a little: my no-iron shirts shifted from one side to the other, my only dress moved to the front.

I proceeded carefully towards the bathroom.

Empty. Intruder-free.

I took a deep breath and lowered the breadboard.

That was when I saw that the top of my laundry basket was on the floor and the black trousers—the ones I'd been wearing when I found Pepe's body, the ones I'd used to wipe my hand, sticky with Pepe's blood—were gone.

I was still trying to process what all this might mean when my phone rang. It was the sheriff.

***

"Thanks for coming down so quickly, Miss... Nickelbaum."

"Always happy to help the law," I said, glancing over at a young woman by the sheriff's desk, who was taking notes on a pad.

"Just for the record, I hope you don't confuse me with Nicholas Nickleby, a character in a novel by that name written by Charles Dickens in the 19th Century."

The sheriff gave me a blank look—and motioned for his stenographer to stop scribbling.

He moved out from behind his desk and sat on the edge.

"I am very concerned about your future here, with us. That you found poor Eddie's dead body under suspicious circumstances—you were wandering around the library after closing time—was unfortunate. But I was willing to accept your story because I couldn't figure out what motive you might have had to murder him.

"But the second murder? That you found another murdered man in the library after hours? What are the odds?"

I shrugged. "If you're about to accuse me of murder, shouldn't I have a lawyer present? And maybe a tape-recorder rather than a stenographer?"

"We still like to do things here in the traditional way. It's more personal. Our stenographer is very highly trained. As for a lawyer, there's no need for that—yet. We're still, I hope, all friends here. I'm merely trying to figure out why and how, our small town, which hadn't had a murder since the nine-teen-twenties—someone running illegal liquor in from the Keys—suddenly has two murders, both in the library, and both discovered by the newest member of the library staff, a recent resident from New York City."

"I didn't have any reason to kill Eddie. I certainly had no reason to kill Pepe. I'm new in town. I don't know what motives others in town might have had to kill these two men. But I'm just the new librarian."

The sheriff nodded. "Sure, sure. And I was about to cross you off any possible list of suspects until I found these in your cabin." He walked back to his desk, reached down and unfurled my blood-stained black trousers. "Do these belong to you?"

I nodded.

"That's a yes, Miss Hatten," he instructed the stenographer before turning to me again. "How do you explain the fact that our lab has found blood stains on the right leg of these trousers that belong to the murdered janitor?"

Even though good sense at this juncture dictated I shut up and get lawyer, I couldn't stop myself from answering. "I was alone in the library, as you say, Sheriff. I heard the sound of a broom and the wheels of the trash can, and I went to see if it was Pepe. When I found his body in the trash receptacle, I was so scared that I had to grab hold of the can to steady myself, and in the process I got some blood on my hands. I must have wiped it off on the leg of my pants."

The sheriff rolled up the pants and put them back behind the desk where he had found them. He reached back into his stash of goodies and extracted the small bottle of ink I had taken from Eddie's office, holding it up in front of me.

"And how do you explain the presence of this half-filled bottle of indelible ink, traces of which were found on Eddie's body?"

I had completely forgotten about taking it. Why had I? I could hardly remember now. As evidence of something against someone, maybe. But now it was being used against me!

I sneezed, half-intentionally stalling for time. "Excuse me." I opened my purse and felt around for a few seconds. "Does anyone have a tissue?"

The sheriff rapped the desk impatiently. The stenographer handed me a tissue from a box in a desk drawer. I dutifully blew my nose.

"The ink bottle," I repeated. "Oh. Yes. The East End light is famous and so many great artists have worked here—William Merritt Chase...Fairfield Porter.... I just thought I would try to sketch a little myself."

"We didn't find any pens. Any sketches."

"None of my sketches were worth saving. I broke the point on the pen. I guess I'm better at words than pictures."

"That ink isn't even used for sketches. It's used for fancy lettering."

"No wonder I made such a mess!" I put the tissue into my purse.

The sheriff grunted and replaced the bottle of ink in his box of evidence. "Well, that's all for now," he said. "I'll need you to sign a statement when it's written up, but you're free to go for now. Please don't plan on leaving Pilgrim's Landing until our investigation is concluded."

I rose from the chair. "Can I please see a copy of the warrant you filed to search my cabin?"

The sheriff nodded to the stenographer to stop taking notes.

"I'll be happy to furnish your lawyer with any documentation he feels necessary when the time comes."

"And what name will I be using to sign this statement? Sandra Nickelbaum?"

"Sandra Nussbaum is the name on record, I do believe."

I gave him a thumbs up and walked towards the door.

"One more thing, Miss Nussbaum," the sheriff said. "You should choose your friends more carefully. People are known by the company they keep. "

He looked me up and down. "You are much too pretty to be wasting your time with Messi. There are far more interesting and...influential men in Pilgrim's Landing."

"I'll take your advice under consideration," I said, and quickly walked out the door.

**

It took a little convincing, but in the end, Ellen agreed to let me come with her to "say a final goodbye" to Eddie's mansion on the cliff at Heaven's Edge.

We were walking around another widow's walk, which seemed like a standard feature of buildings near the water. The view was spectacular.

"Must have been very scary for the wives—looking out to sea and not knowing if they would ever see their husbands again."

Ellen shook her head. "Not these wives. Their husbands were landowners, businessmen—ran the hardware stores, the grocery stores, tackle shops, iron foundries, even the taverns. The architecture was a sham, a nod to a tradition, like the one at the library."

I looked to my left, scanning the cliff. There they were, six, seven, maybe eight large houses hugging the edge like sentinels looking out to sea. To the right, there were fewer, a couple of empty spaces where houses might once have stood.

"That house there," Ellen said, pointing to the closest one, "belongs to Job. The one with that funny tower in the corner—that's where Winston lives. Next to him is the Spencer House. He made his money building railroads. Next over is the Carlson place. They had hundreds of stores all over America that sold buttons, needles, thread and the kind of odds and ends everybody needs."

I pointed to the remains of a house on the right.

"That's the Smith house. Rumor has it Abraham Collins Smith burned it down for the insurance."

"Where I come from it was textile factories that sometimes caught fire. They called it 'Jewish lightning.'"

Ellen laughed. "Whatever. People in Pilgrim's Landing aren't any better than people anywhere else, even though they pretend they are."

Inside, the house looked like a set from a Dickens novel—Miss Havisham's house, to be exact—down to the antique furniture covered in white dust cloths, and cobwebs in every corner.

It seemed to me that time had stood still after Eddie's parents died. Eddie and Ellen avoided the large formal rooms downstairs—the huge living room the dining room and others I didn't even have a name for. They used the kitchen and hung out in a mid-sized wood paneled library and a smaller room off the kitchen that Ellen called, "the breakfast room." These were in tip-top shape and showed Ellen's managing hand.

Upstairs, Eddie's bedroom looked eerily as if he had just left it. The bed was unmade, there were a couple of empty coffee cups on his desk. On the floor near his bed were some dirty socks and a couple of t-shirts.

Ellen paused in the doorway. I felt so bad for her. I wondered if she'd want to touch anything in the room or instead turn it into some kind of shrine. But Ellen had been raised to always do the correct thing, and now she moved quickly towards the bed, began to adjust the covers and fluff up the pillow. She picked up the dirty socks and the empty coffee cups.

I noticed a photograph on the bookshelf of a young woman in soccer gear. Somebody had signed their name boldly at the bottom. As I got closer, I saw that it was "Marna Van Dugan."

I picked up the wooden frame. She was blond, kind of thick in the waist, a wooden shoe away from being Heidi. Her cap said Paradise Center Soccer.

"Marna Van Dugan! Eddie knew her?"

"She was a star on the soccer team in Bliss Bay for a while. That's probably where Eddie met her and Messi. Messi was quite the soccer star in his day. Eddie told me he won the East End championship with a goal off the side of his head, and the coaches of the local high schools showed a video of that shot to all the new kids on the team."

Ellen took the photo out of my hands and replaced it on the shelf. Then she moved around the room, straightening papers on Eddie's desk. She opened and closed a couple of drawers.

"Hello! What's this?" she called out. In the bottom drawer of Eddie's desk, hidden by a dirty T-shirt on the floor, was a locked strong box.

For a minute she hesitated. It was hard enough to go through the most personal possessions of the man you loved, horribly murdered, whose ashes no longer even remained to comfort her. Hard as all this was, she was familiar with most of the items in the house, with Eddie's clothing, even his underwear. But this box? A secret he had kept from her. What might be hidden there?" Love letters from another woman? Pornography? Some kind of sinful behavior he had wanted to keep to himself? A proper Pilgrim would probably choose to bury it in his family plot or throw it into the sea. But Ellen did not want to let any part of Eddie escape her.

She picked up the box and shook it—no sound or anything, really. She laid it on the bed, disappeared downstairs, and returned with a large pair of metal clippers, which she used to cut the lock open. Inside were several files.

The two of us sat on the bed and looked through them. I was hoping Eddie might have made a will, leaving part or all of his fortune to Ellen. No such luck.

What was inside were a number of yellowed pages with faded writing on them. One had an official looking stamp of a pilgrim woman outlined in red and gold ink. Another just had the same signature written several times as if someone were practicing how to reproduce it.

The document I examined looked like a property deed made out to Edmund Needham. I couldn't make out the acreage—it was either 50 or 500. But the signature was clear! It belonged to James Farrett, representing the Earl of Stirling. And the date! The date was clearest of all—1640.

There were a group of papers, held together with a paperclip that looked like maps with outlines of property borders. Several bordered on Lake Minihaha, a large freshwater lake in the area. But while the first map showed five acres bordering the lake belonging to Harriet Dobson Michaels, the next one showed only two acres attributed to Michaels, the rest to Conscience Crossing Realty. Another clipped-together set of maps showed lands owned by the Shinnecock, bordering the bay. This acreage too was redrawn, so that half of it was transferred to Conscience Crossing Realty.

What could it all mean?

Ellen jumped up off the bed and began pacing the room, stopping every few moments to shake the papers at me.

"This is why Eddie was murdered! All those old documents at the library! Someone is forging documents. Not only forging existing documents, but even redrawing boundaries of property! After all—what do all these old people know? When their husbands die, most of them have no idea of how much land they own. I'm a living example of that! My dad always told us he'd won a five-acre plot of land near the town dump in a poker game. He told us never to sell it, it was for a rainy day. But he hid that deed somewhere in our house and only told my mom. Now she has Alzheimer's. I'll probably never find that deed! Eddie must have found out about the forgery ring and threatened to blow the whistle!"

I didn't necessarily share Ellen's view, but I kept my mouth shut. I could still picture Eddie's body, slumped over his computer, blood from his slashed jugular dripping to the floor.

Suddenly, I remembered something else, too. His fingertips black with ink. That bottle of black ink that had turned over and spilled onto the desk.

What had the sheriff said? "That ink is used for fancy lettering."

Ellen was right. Someone connected with the library was forging documents. And it was likely that the sheriff was involved, given the way he'd gone through Eddie's files. I imagined there were hundreds of collectors who would pay top dollar for that sort of document dating back to the 1600s. It further figured that Eddie was into the forgery scheme up to his neck, maybe using his computer skills to scan, copy and create documents very close to the originals.

Of course, now that his body had been cremated, Eddie's role in the scheme couldn't be easily proven. Perhaps with his marriage on the near horizon, Eddie had decided to threaten the others with exposure if he didn't get a bigger piece of the pie. Which is when whoever was his partner decided to get rid of him.

Whether Eddie had been the perpetrator or potential whistle-blower—or both—would probably come to light, eventually. The question was how to proceed.

Since I was now a suspect, and so was Letitia Rose, and nobody trusted the sheriff to do his job properly, where did we go from here?

Ellen and I stared at one another in silence. Almost everyone we could think of was a suspect.

Job had fought in Afghanistan and clearly knew how to use a knife. He would also know where Letitia Rose kept her purse. So that made him a suspect.

Winston had a knife. I had seen him open a box of documents from the old library that he needed for research. He, too, would know where Letitia stashed her own.

The most likely ally would be Hal, the editor of *The Star*. He knew everybody's secrets but didn't like to step on anyone's toes. He would not be eager to bring shame and attention to Pilgrim's Landing.

We knew we needed to gather more evidence. In the meantime, we needed to clean up the rest of Eddie's mansion. We walked around upstairs, the old wooden boards creaking underfoot. There were five more bedrooms on the second floor.

"In the old days, people used to have big families. By the time Eddie was born, it was just him. I don't think these rooms were used much—unless they had a big party and some guests stayed over."

Downstairs, the carpets on the main floor were rolled up and the planks beneath still held their polish. The once white drapes were yellow and streaked with dirt.

I saw a small flash of grey run across the floor and disappear under the sofa.

"A rat! You need to get an exterminator, Ellen. They can really do some damage here."

She shook her head. "There are no rats in Pilgrim's Landing. Everyone knows that. How could a rat climb all the way up the cliff to Eddie's house?"

"How do they climb on ropes to get to ships? This house is right on the bay."

"Must be a field mouse living under the hedges outside."

We walked slowly from room to room, and Ellen's spirits really began to sink.

The house was half-mausoleum, half-shrine, filled with memories and objects from past generations. For the first time, I realized how one can feel suffocated by the burden of one's own history and possessions. Rootless Jew that I was, I could see there was a certain freedom in being an outsider in every culture.

All those dark paintings in heavy gilt frames. Large, hulking pieces of furniture with curved legs and bulging centers—like people with big bellies who had eaten too much.

The house might have been built by the pilgrims who worshipped plain and practical, but the last generation clearly admired the fussy and decorative. All the furniture was French rococo.

Ellen suddenly brightened. She ran over to a dusty rocking-horse in the corner of the room. It had only one eye and there was straw coming out of its belly.

"Crackerjack!" Ellen put her arms around it. "When Eddie and I were kids, we used to take turns riding him. Then one day I tried to give him a treat but all I had were Crackerjacks. Eddie's mom got such a kick out of it that forever after we all called this horse "Crackerjack.""

"Take him. He's yours." I took hold of his front legs and started to pull him towards the middle of the room.

"I can't! It will make me cry!"

"You can. It will make you smile and remember the good times."

We took another turn around the living room.

"Look at this!" Ellen lifted a tarnished coffee pot from an antique sideboard decorated with marquetry and edged with gilt.

"Grandma Hayden's table and coffee set. I remember Eddie's mom pouring me a cup of tea from it one Christmas."

Ellen lifted up a small creamer and wiped it on her jeans. "Lookie here. Just needs a little polish. It's a beauty!"

"Take it! It's yours!"

Ellen shook her head.

"I can't take it. It would be so out of place in my house."

"Nonsense. Eddie would have wanted you to have it. Take it. It's a gift from his house to yours. Even cousin Abigail would want you to have it!"

I reached for the coffee pot and started to cram it into my purse.

Ellen grabbed my arm. "You can't treat an antique like that!"

She carefully replaced the coffeepot on the tray, went into the kitchen, and returned with several kitchen towels and a large canvas bag. Then she wordlessly wrapped up the coffee set, tray, creamer, sugar bowl, one small silver spoon and said, "Are you satisfied now? I'll take it home."

I gave her a hug. "Let's see what's in the kitchen."

The room was as big as my entire apartment on Fifth Avenue. I wandered around, opening and closing drawers and cabinets. I lifted up a couple of forks and spoons. "Take a look at this! Must be a service for fifty here! This sterling is worth a fortune!"

Ellen peered over my shoulder, picked up a couple of forks and spoons and put them back. Then she shut the drawer.

I opened one of the glass cabinets. It was filled with white porcelain plates, trimmed with gold. The same number of settings, from the looks of it, as the silver. Ellen shook her head and wordlessly closed the cabinet. "I don't want the silver. I don't want the dishes! All I want is my Eddie back!"

She sat down on a stool and started to cry.

I knelt down and put my arms around her. I started to drag the horse towards the door.

"I think we've done enough. We'll leave the rest of the cleanup to a service."

Ellen suddenly stood up, wiped her tears on the sleeve of her shirt. "Cleaning Service! In my Eddie's house?"

"Yes—a cleaning service. They should have been called eons ago!"

Then we dragged the horse and the silver coffee set to the car, and Ellen drove me home.

CHAPTER EIGHT

"...if truth were everywhere to be shown, a scarlet letter would blaze forth on many a bosom...."

—**Nathaniel Hawthorne,** *The Scarlet Letter*

I didn't believe Messi was involved in profiting from forged historical documents, but I also doubted he'd want to take part in rounding up any of the profiteers in Pilgrim's Landing or get mixed up with some lunatic serial murderer—especially since some of his own activities might not bear scrutiny by the law. The fact is, I was pretty sure Messi cared more about keeping his own sweet ass out of trouble than rescuing a bunch of people he didn't know very well from a stuck-up town that didn't hold him in high regard.

It was not all that different, in the end, from the rules of the jungle that was New York City. You didn't turn in your friends, but you didn't sacrifice yourself for them either. The only difference was the mask people wore was only one layer thick in New York, whereas here it went back generations. Like the skin of an onion, peel off one layer and you'd find another layer underneath.

But it turned out I was wrong about Messi's priorities and him not caring if it wasn't his ass on the line.

"Letitia Rose a killer? No way. She may be a snob, but she's certainly not a killer. That knife belonged to her dad. Got it off a dead soldier in Vietnam. Lots of people knew about her knife and watched her cut open those cartons of books."

"I don't think the sheriff thinks she killed anyone. She's just a suspect. Me too."

I gave Messi a short summary of my bloody pants story, skipping over my meeting with the phony ghost on the roof of the library—a figure straight out of *Hamlet*. If my best friend Ellen thought it was a dream or hallucination, I wasn't taking any chances with Messi. The last thing I wanted was for him to dismiss me as a hysterical female.

"The sheriff! That man's really beginning to get on my nerves. Remember, I told you that I pick my fights? I think maybe the sheriff needs a lesson in 'correctness.' I got a couple of ideas. Does the library still do photo exhibitions?"

"Yes. There's something up now, a bunch of sailboats and flowers. Not too impressive."

"We can put on a much better show than that. In the meantime, get into your bathing suit. We're going to do a little night fishing!"

Night fishing! It was strange how just the sound of Messi's voice excited me. I put on a two-piece bathing suit that was real easy to slip on and off—in case the occasion arose—and this time I planned ahead a little and took a change of clothes: a pair of jeans, underwear and a clean T-shirt that read: Shakespeare Lives!

It was dusk when Messi picked me up in his beat-up Volkswagen bug. I drew a peace sign in lipstick on the side window and felt as if I had shed 25 years.

We'd just driven past the Pilgrim's Landing town line when a policeman pulled us over.

Messi didn't say a word.

I tried to follow suit, but couldn't keep my mouth shut. "Excuse me, officer, can you please tell me why you pulled us over?"

The kid—he couldn't have been more than 19, complete with adolescent pimples—peered into the front seat.

"Sorry, Messi. Driver's license?"

Messi pulled his license from his pocket. "Not a problem."

The kid didn't even look at it. Just wrote something in his ticket book, tore it out and handed it to Messi.

"Warning. Going below speed limit can cause accidents."

The kid tipped his cap and moved back to his car.

Messi put the car in gear.

"Just a little local harassment," Messi said. "Happens every week or so. I suspect it'll stop very soon."

Messi stepped on the gas. "Look at that sunset!"

And I did.

***

I left my clothes on a rock by the shore below the cliff where Messi's house was perched. It was like an eagle's nest, positioned on the crest, with a commanding view of all below. We climbed into his dingy, tipping this way and that in the shallows. Messi rowed us out to his fishing boat, which was moored about a quarter mile from shore.

I flung my flipflops onboard. With the other hand, I grabbed hold of a rung of the small ladder on the side of the boat and tried pulling myself up. It was a struggle, the boat yawing side to side, but Messi steadied and lifted me, a strong hand under my bottom, and I swung myself over the side.

"Gotta work up those muscles, girl." He scampered up behind me, pulled out a couple of long fishing rods, and set them up in some brackets in the stern. Then he took the lid off a metal container filled with what looked like cut up pieces of fish (ugh), which he began threading on the fishing hooks.

I seated myself as far away from him as possible while this slimy activity was going on and tried to concentrate on the streaks of red coloring the horizon and turning the clouds soft pink. Still, the hook-baiting was hard to ignore.

"What are we fishing for, exactly?" I asked.

"Blues. They're running now."

"Where are they running?"

"It just means there's a lot of 'em around."

"What are you using for bait?"

"They'll go for anything shiny, even the artificial stuff. But I like bait. Mullet, mackerel, eels, squid, shrimp. Doesn't much matter whether it's dead or alive either."

He disappeared into the bowels of the boat and returned with a bottle of wine, two wine glasses, and a couple of mats, which he laid out in the back of the boat. He put the two glasses down next to him and beckoned me down beside him. For a few minutes we just lay there together, our arms entwined, staring up at the sky.

Still no invitation to visit below. "This boat. Does it have a name?"

"Of course. She's Diana."

"Goddess of the moon."

Messi laughed. "Diana was my mother's name. And she was a goddess. She died when I was ten, but she taught me to swim."

"It's a little too early to drop our lines. The blues really get going when the moon comes out. In the meantime, I thought we could find some other ways to entertain ourselves."

He managed to open the wine with a flick of his knife, then he poured us each a healthy amount and held up his glass.

"It seems to me you don't travel as light as you let on at your house," I said.

"That's my house," he said. "This is my home." He clinked my glass. "*C'ent anni!*"

"Doesn't that mean 'one hundred years?' And isn't that usually a birthday toast?"

"Miss Librarian, you really do know everything! It's true about *C'ent anni*. Even though I grew up in Sands End, I really didn't learn that much Italian. In bygone days every little kid wanted to be American. 'Course I'm sorry now, but I do remember some Italian stuff."

He leaned in and kissed me. "There are some things Italians are born knowing."

"I'll say."

"Come on," he said, getting up and pulling me to my feet. "I'm going to give you a tour of my home, but first I need to school the city girl so she can start using the proper terminology for things. Can't have you out at sea without knowing the language—the names we give things inside a fishing boat. Now, look in front of you. That's the bow of the boat."

He turned me around.

"And that's the stern—what a landlubber would call the rear end."

He took my arm and led me towards the front—oops—the bow of the boat.

"Now we're moving aft, away from the bow, towards the back—the stern—and the walls on the side, those are called the bulkheads. The right side is starboard. The left is port. And this," he said, pointing at what looked like a large hutch, "is the wheelhouse." There wasn't much to see there. A steering wheel and a few dials and what looked like some sort of lever with a plastic handle.

"Here's a trick that might make things easier for you to remember. Do you know where the word *posh* came from?"

I shook my head.

"When all the rich English guys went to India to enslave the natives, the best cabins were on the right side, facing land instead of the boring sea. On the way back to England, the best cabins were on the left side facing land, so *posh* came to mean port out, starboard home."

Messi put his arms around me and turned me around. "Port left."

He turned me around again. "Starboard right."

I stared out into the water. No land on either side. I wasn't interested in land at the moment. I wanted to see more of the boat. There really wasn't much to see aft either. Just more room back here, a white-washed deck that looked pretty clean. What I really wanted to see was inside. Where he got the wine and glasses.

I pointed to the stairs. "What's down there?"

"The cabin."

He held on to me—it was a little tricky going down the narrow, canted steps with one hand holding a glass of wine and the boat bobbing up and down.

Downstairs, it was all polished wood. It looked just like those ads you see in magazines. There was a narrow bunk bed on one side with a plain khaki-color blanket, tight as the one in his house on the cliff. There were a few pillows, one in a faded shade of indigo, another in a South Seas blue and yellow floral print. Lots of small drawers and cubby-holes.

No photos.

But a number of very interesting ashtrays: a blue and white one next to the bed in the shape of a dog. On the side it said "Salty Dog Café, Key West. Another, on the other side of the bed was pink and shaped like a boat. That one said, Dos Hermanos, Cuba. Across the room on a small shelf, there were two more, one in the shape of a sombrero, with the name Sol Y Luna, Tijuana, Mexico. And the other, in the shape of the Coliseum, marked Roma, Italia.

On a small table in front of the bunk bed was a cigar box. The name on the box was Montecristo no. 2. This was a name I recognized. The most expensive Cuban cigars. Legally unavailable in the U.S. I know, because my ex-husband paid large sums under the table to various people whose business it was to smuggle them in.

I opened the box. Sure enough—it was filled with cigars, laid out in neat rows. Was Messi a heavy smoker? I knew he rolled a joint from time to time—but I had never smelled nicotine on his breath.

He came up behind me and wordlessly shut the box.

He led me toward the kitchen.

"This we call the galley."

Here there were shelves of bottled spices, a large pepper-grinder, several strainers, wooden spoons, an electric blender, a wooden rack of chef's knives, pots hanging off hooks of all different sizes, a wooden wine rack.

I opened one drawer and saw a garlic press, two wine-openers, a vegetable scrapper, a cheese grater. I opened one of the overhead doors and found a number of plates, mugs, glasses, silverware, even a gravy boat—in the shape of a boat, of course.

"So, you like to cook?"

"I'm Italian. Of course, I cook. How about you? Jews love food, too."

"Jews love food, but some of us—me—would rather eat than cook. I'm a working woman. Not much time—or space in that little cottage—to cook much of anything."

"Really now. I'm going to cook you up something right here that'll blow away all your excuses."

Right. At least they would be cooked clams instead of raw ones.

And then I saw two other ashtrays on a shelf above the stove. One said, Grand Hotel, Casa Blanca, Morocco. The other, Hotel Miramar, Istanbul, Turkey.

Either Messi was a really heavy smoker, or something else was going on here.

I reached over and picked up the Moroccan ashtray. "Did you buy any rugs when you were here?"

Messi smiled and gently took the ashtray out of my hands. "Don't think I had enough money to buy a rug when I was there."

He turned me around and pointed to a small door.

"That's one of the most important rooms—the bathroom. We call it the head."

I opened the door. No ashtrays in here. I opened the medicine cabinet. A razor and a couple of razor blades. Two toothbrushes and a tube of toothpaste. No drugs, pills, syringes, not even condoms. I wasn't sure if I was relieved or disappointed. The Moroccan connection was a surprise. At one time that was where most of the illicit drugs came from. Was Messi smuggling drugs into the U.S.? It certainly looked like he was smuggling Cuban cigars.

We went back on deck and settled down on the mats he had rolled out earlier. He pointed to another area, near the bow.

"That's the hold. Just contains lots of fishing stuff, like nets, hooks, bait. "

And then he kissed me, longer and better.

For a while we lay there together again, our bodies touching, looking out on the sea and sipping wine, Messi thinking who knows what, me wondering if Messi was a killer, dope fiend, smuggler, or all of the above.

And then I saw a great white bird settle on top of the steering wheel. "Oh, my God. Is that an Albatross?"

"Sorry to say, just a rather large seagull. They get pretty fat out here."

He picked up a clam shell and tossed it at the bird, which quickly flew away.

I couldn't resist showing off. I told him that after Ismael had killed the albatross, he was punished because he'd killed one of God's creatures. I recited from a Coleridge poem:

"I looked to heaven, and tried to pray,

But ere even a prayer had gushed,

A wicked whisper came and made

My heart as dry as dust.

"That's from The Ancient Mariner, by Coleridge."

Messi chuckled. "You know, you tell me stuff about *The Old Man and the Sea* and *The Ancient Mariner*—all those lies we learned in school. The real truth is there are no ancient mariners, or old men who go to sea. They all die young."

He sat up and poured himself another glass of wine.

"My father drowned in a hurricane at sea; my grandfather was killed by a mast that broke off during a storm; his father before him was becalmed for weeks and died of thirst and exposure."

I shivered. The wind was picking up but maybe it was just that I was getting upset hearing him talk like this.

"That's so awful," I said, nuzzling against him. "Why did you become a fisherman, knowing all that?"

"I didn't choose the sea. The sea chose me. I was born on board my father's boat in the middle of a hurricane. My father cut my umbilical cord with the same knife I use to gut the fish I catch."

"Did you really manage to keep afloat for four days, hanging on to a pair of rubber boots?"

"Sometimes you have to improvise. I didn't have many options."

"Ellen told me some people in town think you can breathe underwater."

He laughed. "Only when I need to."

He pulled me up to a standing position and drew me close. "All life begins in the sea. That's one truth my father taught me. So, let's make love in the sea."

He pulled his shirt over his head and tossed it on the deck. Then he tugged his bathing suit down off his legs and stepped free. Did the same for me, peeling off my bikini like he was shucking an oyster.

"Hold tight!" he instructed, slinging me over his back. He jumped off the side of the boat, with me clinging to him like I was the cape on a superhero. We plunged down through the wet shock of it together.

For a moment, submerged under water, I felt totally helpless, more frightened than I had ever been in my life. Then Messi dove under me, lifted me high out of the water, and tossed me in again.

He was over me and under me, one minute pulling me down under the water, the next lifting me up.

"I told you we would make love in the sea," he whispered in my ear.

And then we did.

Or rather, we did something.

I wouldn't call it love. It was more like some ancient initiation ritual—some crazy dance—in which Neptune was an active partner.

There were three of us in that ocean, frolicking together in some strange, frenzied mixture of joy, ferocity and tenderness. We were floating on top of each other and diving under each other, splashing in fun and then in fury, chasing each other like dolphins at play.

Messi's legs were longer, but I could change direction more quickly; he was stronger, but I was more flexible and could easily evade capture, and so we played, circled, chased each other, closer companions in the sea than on the land—coming together at last in an unforgettable underwater embrace.

When it was all over, I felt so exhausted Messi had to carry me up the ladder back into the boat. We lay down together once more on the padded mats. Within minutes, Messi's regular breathing told me he was asleep, but I lay there, staring up into the now finally dark sky for some time, only the moon and the stars providing any light. Who was Messi? God? Devil? Pirate? One thing seemed sure. He was more than a man. He was an energy force.

I must have finally fallen asleep because the next thing I remember was a cold, wet slap across my face. "What in hell....?"

All around me on the deck were squirming fins and tails, their iridescent colors glittering in the moonlight.

Bluefish!

The deck was full of them. And there was Messi, holding on to one of the fishing poles, bent almost in half with the weight on the end of the hook.

When he heard me, he reeled in the fish he'd hooked, netted it, and set the rod back in its holder. Truth is, he didn't need the rod. The fish were jumping into the boat by themselves!

"Look! Look over there!" He pointed down into the water.

Beneath us, the water was boiling with bluefish. They flashed in the moonlight, fins cutting through the water.

"What are you? A magician? A fish whisperer? I can't believe this!"

"No magic at all. I just followed the birds. I saw them heading out this way earlier in the day. They follow the food and I follow them."

"What are you going to do with so many fish?"

Messi looked at the fish flopping and smacking on the deck. "Right now, we're going to head for shore, and you're gonna be careful not to lose a toe. These fuckers are vicious, and their teeth are sharp."

He went back to the front of the boat and started the mechanism that pulled up the anchor.

"There are a few restaurants I deal with who will take them off my hands. Have you ever eaten fresh bluefish?"

He picked one up by its tail and dangled it in front of me. "I'll give you $100 if you eat this fish!"

I shook my head.

"You really won't eat fish?"

"I didn't say I wouldn't eat fish. I said I wouldn't eat fish for money."

"For what then?"

I stared at him. "What else do you have to trade?"

"Pleasure. Have I not given you any pleasure?"

I nodded. "Sure. But giving pleasure comes easily to you. I'd like some information."

Messi sat down beside me. "That depends on what you want to know."

I ran my hand over his stomach, and felt a rough patch of skin, scar tissue I hadn't noticed before. It stopped above his crotch.

"Where'd you get these scars?"

"I went too far out on my surfboard, and a shark took a nibble."

"A couple of inches lower would not have been good."

"Something for which I have been eternally grateful."

"That makes two of us."

Messi ran his fingers gently through my hair. "Where'd you get that white streak in your hair?"

"From my dad. He was born with it. I was born with it."

"It looks like a streak of lightning. Like Wonder Woman."

"Little known fact: She was invented by an American psychologist inspired by a woman fighting for women's rights and sexual equality. Only problem was, he fell in love with the woman. He told his wife he would divorce her unless she accepted his girlfriend into their home—so for many years they had a ménage a trois."

"A *ménage a trois?*" He had two women at once?"

"Does that tickle your fancy?"

"At this point in my life, I prefer my women one at a time."

I moved closer. He had a small tattoo of an anchor over his bellybutton. I ran my fingers over its smooth surface.

"I've never been with a man who has a tattoo."

"And I've never been with a woman who talks so much in bed."

I ran my hand over the muscles of his chest. Suddenly, I had the kind of intuitive feeling only a crazy city-bred woman like me was likely to have. And before I could stop my mouth, I had blurted out, "Have you ever been in jail?"

I felt him stiffen. Then he got to his feet. "I think we've traded enough for one evening—besides, I've got to get the blues to the restaurants early this morning."

He started the motor and took the wheel. We said very little to each other until we tied up to the mooring. Messi lowered me into the dingy and rowed us to the shore below his house.

Once more, I saw the shallow waters nearby, alive with the movement of people and splashing water. There were murmured greetings. Hawkeye emerged from the shadows.

"Any blues out there?"

"A whole bunch. I put 'em on ice. I'll deliver them as soon as I drop this lady off. Come on," Messi said to me. "Let me drive you home." He helped me out of the dingy and led me up a winding path to the nook in the woods, where he parked his car.

When we reached my cottage, he kissed me again and held me close.

"Stop doing so much research into my past, Miss Librarian. You might not like what you find."

Then he got into his car and took off without a backward glance.

***

Notes from Sandra, Assistant Librarian

Bluefish: Pomatomus saltatrix

Class: Actinop Terygil

Phylum: Chordate

Taste: Possibly edible, if cooked and accompanied with some kind of sauce and lots of garlic

CHAPTER NINE

"Flow on river! Flow with the floodtide, and ebb with the ebb-tide!

Frolic on, crested and scallop-edg'd waves!

Gorgeous clouds of the sunset! Drench with your splendor me, or the men and women generations after me!"

—**Walt Whitman**, *On Crossing Brooklyn Ferry*

"Good morning, Miss Nussbaum," Letitia Rose's voice chirped happily over the phone. "Holiday's over. The library will open today at noon. They found the killer!"

For a minute I felt elated, like a huge weight had been lifted. No more fear of a lunatic killer prowling the halls of the library.

"Who was it? A drifter? Or someone we know?"

"Jose Ortiz, one of the Mexican kids who hang out at the library. Pepe's nephew."

Pepe's nephew? Jose Ortiz. The kid who was reading Winnie-the-pooh? A murderer? No way. Uh uh. Nah. It didn't take Sherlock Holmes to know what the sheriff was up to. He needed a fall guy. A pigeon. Somebody to pin the blame on. Someone who none of the good people of Pilgrim's Landing would even miss. Even Miss Correctness herself, Letitia Rose, considered the Mexican kids second-class citizens—if citizens at all.

And anyway, why would Pepe's nephew want to murder his uncle with a knife belonging to Letitia Rose? He was such a weak, skinny kid—I couldn't imagine him overpowering a stray cat, let alone a hefty fellow like Pepe.

I jumped in the shower, then put on my black trousers and white shirt, my library uniform, got on my bike and cycled over to the library.

The yellow crime-scene tape had been removed. Ellen was behind the front desk. Letitia Rose bustled up and down the aisles between the bookshelves, moving books that had been misplaced to their correct location.

The door behind me opened—the postman delivering two cartons of new books.

"Sheriff give you back your knife yet?"

"He most certainly did not! When Job comes in later, he'll have to open those boxes."

I slid in behind the desk and sat next to Ellen. "How in hell did the sheriff get this kid so fast?"

"Seems the police found Eddie's wallet on him. "

"So, he killed Eddie and Pepe?"

Ellen shrugged. "You know these illegals...I can't tell you how many times I bought this kid a sandwich. I always pegged him for an addict. It's rampant in the Mexican community. Alcohol for the Indians, opioids for the Mexicans."

Nothing in the story made sense to me. If the kid robbed Eddie's wallet, why didn't he take his watch? I distinctly remember seeing it on his wrist after he was murdered.

And why would the kid kill his uncle? I couldn't imagine he had anything valuable enough to lead someone to murder him.

The only thing I could think of was he might have killed Pepe because Pepe saw him kill Eddie. But what reason would this strung-out Mexican kid have to kill Eddie?

Besides, when poor Pepe had given me his little silver cross, he said, "Mal hombre." Bad man. Jose was barely sixteen. I knew enough Spanish to think that Pepe would have said, "mal hijo." And if the killer was his nephew, why would he think I needed a cross for protection?

"If the kid was a robber, why didn't he steal Eddie's watch? Eddie was still wearing it when I found him. Come to think of it, whatever happened to that watch?"

Ellen shook her head. "I don't know anything about Eddie's watch. Eddie really loved that watch. It was his fathers and his fathers before that. "

I had seen the Sheriff's deputy grab Eddie's wrist to take his pulse. I had seen the light of Eddie's lamp bounce off the metal of the gold band. The only one who could have stolen Eddie's watch and wallet was the sheriff! It was no wonder he'd needed a patsy.

But what could I do from here? I wasn't sure how much I could depend on Letitia Rose to leave her bias behind even though she didn't trust the sheriff.

I slid out from behind the big desk and motioned for Letitia Rose to take a seat with me at one of the oak reading tables.

"There's a problem here. Bill Bronson is trying to pin these murders on that poor boy who has no one to protect him. Bronson just needs some quick, convenient solution to these murders to make himself look good. He doesn't give a damn about justice. Besides, I think there's a good chance that there's some forgery ring operating out of this library and the sheriff is covering for them."

"In my library! A forgery ring! Bite your tongue, girl! That could never be. Whoever said that is a rat-faced liar!"

Letitia Rose regarded her library the way a priest regards his cathedral.

"I'll tell you everything later. Right now we need to prevent that sheriff from blaming a murder on that innocent boy!"

Letitia Rose made some "tsk, tsk" noises and shook her head. "But he found evidence on that boy. He found Eddie's wallet. I don't like Bill Bronson at all—at all—you hear me? But he found real evidence on that boy."

"I don't think anyone robbed Eddie except the sheriff or his deputy. I saw Eddie's gold watch on his wrist when I found the body. That watch was on his wrist when the sheriff and his deputy came to retrieve the body. If that boy stole the wallet, why didn't he take the watch?"

Letitia Rose took a deep breath. "What happened to that watch? That watch belonged to Eddie's father and Eddie's grandfather. Isn't anyone in town could wear that watch without half the town knowing whose watch it was. Unless—unless he sold it to someone in New York City!"

She rose majestically from the chair. "I think it is time that some of us here at Pilgrim's Landing did something about that sheriff. And don't you give that Mexican boy any more worry. He will have plenty of friends in Pilgrim's Landing."

Letitia Rose got out her iPhone and stepped outside, obeying her own rules of quiet in the reading room. I saw her wandering around the library the rest of the afternoon. I didn't know exactly who she else she called, but she invited me to a little "Shaming Session" that evening at six at Mohicans Bar.

I wondered if Messi would be there. I wondered if I should invite him. But I decided that his relationship with the sheriff was already so toxic, I should let it alone. Besides, I knew Messi was planning to deal with the sheriff himself through some kind of photography exhibition at the library. From what I was slowly finding out, the sheriff of Pilgrim's Landing had more enemies than friends.

***

Messi was not at Mohican's, but Hal, the editor of the *Pilgrim's Landing Star*, was there, along with Hawkeye, Letitia Rose, Ellen, Job and Winston.

Job was entirely at home here. I didn't know about Winston. I saw him pat his back pocket when he entered. It was where he kept his flask. After we took a table in the rear, Hal ordered a round of Guinness for the table, plus an extra one for the sheriff.

I noticed that Hawkeye had his camera and sat as close to Hal as possible.

Hal motioned to us all to be seated. "Now, you all just settle down and follow my lead. We will show Miss Nussbaum here how Pilgrim's Landing justice takes place."

I took a seat next to Ellen. "Are there any official judges or lawyers in Pilgrim's Landing?"

There was a general chuckle. "We are all judges here," Hal said. "Bill Bronson can argue his own case in the court of public opinion."

Winston patted my arm. "I was once a lawyer many years ago, but we try to dispense with them as much as possible. We do things here more by tradition than law, my dear."

As if I didn't already know that.

And then the door opened, and Bill Bronson came in.

I think when he saw us all sitting there, he wanted to turn and run, but it was too late for that—too many of the regulars had already seen him. He nodded to a few people he knew and made his way back to our table. As soon as he was seated, Hawkeye snapped his photograph.

"Didn't know you were all coming. I would have invited my wife."

Hal smiled and patted him on the back. "It's just us tonight. Perhaps another time."

Hal moved to the head of the table and offered a toast: "To Sheriff Bill Bronson, who never lets us down."

We all raised our glasses and Hawkeye took another photograph. There were some calls of "Hear! Hear!" and then we all turned our attention to Hal.

"Well now. I think your wife will be able to read all about our celebration in tomorrow's *Star*. We all just wanted the opportunity to thank you for capturing that murderer so quickly. Saves the town a lot of embarrassment and boosts our business, this being tourist season and all."

Hal looked around the table and we all nodded dutifully while Bill Bronson took a long swallow of his beer.

"Now there are just a few things we wanted to clear up that were a bit puzzling to some of us. What led you to suspect this Mexican boy in the first place?"

The sheriff beamed. "It's no secret these illegal Mexicans—wetbacks my dad used to call'em—are causing problems. Some of them actually swim here from their hellhole to pollute our town. Oh, they start out good enough, picking strawberries, washing dishes, doing yard work and the like, but pretty soon they're stealing, taking drugs, who knows what else. I happen to know this particular kid, Jose Ortiz. He's Pepe's cousin or nephew or something, and he comes to the library for some free food and a roof over his head when it's raining. And I *know* that he's an opioid addict."

Job raised his hand. "How do you know that?"

The sheriff smiled. "Come on. Everyone knows everything in this town. Paul Jenkins, the pharmacist, told me. He's been giving him some other stuff to help him get off it."

I jumped up. "That's a violation of privacy. That's against the law!"

"Excuse me," the Sheriff said, "I know of no such law in Pilgrim's Landing."

Of course not. Everyone already knew everyone else's business. But something else suddenly occurred to me. The sheriff had cooked up a reason to arrest Jose, but it was possible his motive was much more devious. If the sheriff was covering up for the real murderer, and Pepe was killed because he had seen too much about the forgery ring, maybe the Sheriff feared Pepe had spilled the beans to his nephew. Charging Jose with murder got another possible witness out of the way.

Hal picked up his hand. "So where in his house did you find Eddie's wallet?"

"Would you believe it was in plain sight, right on top of his dresser?"

"Did you find the keys to Eddie's office?" Ellen asked. "I understand the outside door was locked."

The sheriff shook his head. "Not yet—still searching the place."

"Did you have a warrant?" I called out.

The sheriff glared at me. "What is this person doing here? She doesn't know what she's talking about. I don't need no permit to go into some wetback's house and arrest him!"

"And my Eddie's watch. Did you find Eddie's watch in that house?"

The sheriff shook his head. "Sorry, Ellen, I know that was Eddie's grandfather's watch. These vermin must have sold it before we got to him."

"Well now, I'm afraid there's a problem there," Letitia Rose said. "Miss Nussbaum here, who discovered poor Eddie's body, says he was wearing the watch when she found him."

The sheriff took another swallow of his beer and began to cough. When he was finished, he glared at me.

"Miss Nussbaum is clearly mistaken. The door was locked when we arrived. The only light came from a small lamp on Eddie's desk. Miss Nussbaum wears glasses, and is quite near-sighted, if I'm not mistaken. I am quite sure she could not have seen a watch on Eddie's wrist, if there was one."

I got up and moved closer to the sheriff. "I see perfectly well with my glasses on. I saw the glint of gold in the light of the lamp."

"I don't know what you imagined you saw, Miss Nussbaum, but I took a long statement from you, following our meeting at the library and you did not mention anything about seeing a watch. Why would a robber take a wallet and leave a watch? Miss Nussbaum is clearly mistaken."

Letitia Rose stood up. "I'm not quite sure about that Bill Bronson. Miss Nussbaum here took a photo with her iPhone when she found the body. Eddie was still wearing his watch when you and your deputy entered. What happened to that watch?"

This literally knocked the sheriff off his feet, and he fell back into his chair, shaking his head but saying nothing.

I must admit that I almost fell out of my chair as well because I had not taken my iPhone down to the lower level of the library that night, and I had no such photograph.

Hal got to his feet and put his arm around Bill Bronson's shoulder. "Now Bill, you and I go back a long way. We've run lots of nasty people out of town.

You're one of our own, and I know I speak for all of us when I say we have no need to share any of what has been said here with anyone else. We know that sometimes evidence, personal items, get lost somewhere between the scene of a crime and the sheriff's office. Can happen to anyone.

"If you say robbery was the motive for the murders, I will print that in tomorrow's *Star*. But I would like some assurance that you'll search for Eddie's grandfather's gold watch and that you will succeed in finding it."

The sheriff nodded his head and finished his beer. He was about to get up when Hal pulled him back into his chair.

"One more thing. This Mexican addict. I think you made a mistake when you said you found Eddie's wallet on his dresser. Maybe it was another wallet that just looked like Eddie's? That poor boy had no reason to kill his uncle or Eddie. In fact, how could such a skinny, weak kid murder a strong man like Eddie? Or Pepe, for that matter.

"Isn't it much more likely that some drifter—a daytripper from New Jersey or someone like that—wandered into the library and tried to rob Eddie? When Eddie put up a fight, the robber stabbed him. Looks to me like maybe that person was scared off in the middle of his crime, interrupted by someone in the hallway. Could have been our own Miss Nussbaum here, searching for some information from Winston in the Research Department?"

The sheriff sat in his chair and stared straight ahead, saying nothing.

Hal nodded and said,

"I think I speak for all of us when I say that your time would be better spent trying to find the real killer. We wouldn't want people in our town to think you were trying to cover up for someone else by pinning these murders on a poor, sick Mexican boy."

Job moved away from the table and rolled up close to the Sheriff. "Quite frankly, I find your handling of this entire situation disgusting."

That was when Winston motioned to the waitress and ordered a double scotch.

At last, the sheriff rose. He glared at each one of us in turn. "Are you finished yet?"

Letitia Rose said, "Not entirely. Where's my knife, Bill Bronson? I want my knife!"

The Sheriff straightened his back. "Whatever you all say about this Mexican being innocent—someone is goddamned guilty, and that person used the knife belonging to Letitia Rose Jefferson to murder that janitor. And one more thing: We looked at the hard drive of Eddie's computer. What we found there could embarrass a number of people in this town! "

Job rose from his seat. "What are you suggesting?"

"I can't discuss these things in front of the ladies."

And with those words, Bill Bronson, sheriff of Pilgrim's Landing, walked out of Mohican's bar.

***

The next morning, the Pilgrim's Landing *Star* had a front-page photo of all of us, raising a glass to Sheriff Bill Bronson. The headline read: "Sheriff Bill Bronson Recovers Stolen Watch and Wallet of Murder-Victim Edmund Rolland Smith. The perpetrator believed to be a day-tripper from New Jersey—has not yet been apprehended."

This was followed by a photo of Ellen holding the newly recovered watch and her statement, "I am much indebted to the fine work of Sheriff Bill Bronson who recovered this beloved family heirloom."

Messi carried his copy of the *Star* and stopped into the library later in the afternoon to offer his congratulations to Letitia, Ellen and me.

"Glad to see some people in this town still have balls."

Letitia laughed. "Yes, sir, and some of us are women."

I stared at Ellen, but she displayed no visible sign of discomfort. But I felt bad for her. It seemed to me she was losing more and more. Not only losing the love of her life, but now having to cope with a somewhat tarnished view of him.

A friend told me her therapist had said, "Everyone has a public life, a private life, and a secret life. Did Eddie have a secret life to be ashamed of, or did the sheriff just make it up in the moment, the way Letitia Rose made up my iPhone photo of Eddie's watch?

No one on the "shaming committee" seemed up to addressing Bill Bronson's veiled threat about exposing material too sensitive to be discussed in front of women. To me, that meant Eddie was probably looking at pornography. Or possibly had some online relationship with a mystery woman.

Eddie didn't seem to me to be the type to have a hidden life, but maybe he was exactly the type who went for that stuff. Too shy to approach most women. A long-term relationship with a respectable woman he planned one day to marry. Everyone, it seems, needed a little excitement in their lives.

I could see how the sheriff managed to hang on to his job. He was both a thief and a bully, but he knew so many secrets about so many people in town no one had the courage to push for his removal.

Even Messi was shocked when I suggested life would be simpler if the town just fired the guy.

"Fire the sheriff? We couldn't do that! He's held that office for 20 years. How can we suddenly admit we've been wrong all this time? Besides, he knows too much about where the bodies are buried to risk antagonizing him. It's like what Lyndon Johnson once said about keeping J. Edgar Hoover in his position as head of the FBI: "I'd rather have him inside the tent, pissing out, than outside the tent, pissing in."

"But he was talking about an entire Congress. I'm only talking about a few townsfolk who work in a small-town library. What could Bill Bronson have on Letitia Rose?"

"Letitia Rose!"

"Or Job?"

"Job!"

We were sitting on a bench in front of the library, and I was really getting mad.

"What is that? I ask you a question you don't want to answer, and that's how you answer it?"

"I just don't want to get into it. The truth about many things and people in this town is very complicated, and I'd rather go fishing."

Me too, but now that the cat was out of the bag about Eddie's "complicated life," I thought it was our duty to seriously consider what Bill Bronson had actually found on Eddie's computer.

Could he have been carrying on an affair with someone in town who decided to murder him when she—or possibly he—found out he was soon to marry Ellen?

Messi laughed at that idea.

"Come on, Miss Librarian. I bet half the men in town have stuff like that on their computer. Nobody confuses those relationships with real life. They are only exciting because they are secret."

"And what do you have on your computer that might be too sensitive to discuss?"

"I'm not that into fantasy. I prefer the real thing."

And with that, he took my arm and pulled me after him, back into the library.

"If we fire Bronson, we might get someone worse. There are lots of ways of keeping him in line, and one of them is by posting a real photograph, not one Letitia Rose invented. "

"And just what is so significant about the photo you have in mind?"

"You'll see soon enough. You know the expression 'one photograph is worth a thousand words?'"

He approached Letitia Rose. "I think it would be a really good time to mount a photographic exhibit in the main hall," he said to her in a lowkey voice. "I know the library offers a course in photography. Does Winston still teach it? Or Job? It's summer and the sunsets are so gorgeous on the East End. Let's announce a contest of some sort. Hal can put it in next week's *Star*. That will give everyone in town something else to think about, instead of murders."

Letitia Rose smiled. "I knew it was a good thing to give you a library card even though you really live in Sands End. I'm sure Hal will be happy to oblige. Shall we give them all two weeks?"

"Two weeks will be just fine." Messi turned and threw me a kiss before walking out the door.

***

One of the lessons I was learning about Pilgrim's Landing was that the Puritan practice of public shaming, wherein people were placed in stockades and spit on and pelted with rotten fruit and worse, had now turned into a private shaming. Or, rather, semi-private shaming. The town crier, who now seemed to be Hal, the editor of the *Pilgrim's Landing Star*, decided what would be "news" and what would not. It was therefore no great surprise to me to learn that I was now heralded as "Pilgrim's Landing's Own Mermaid" with a full-page story and photos, while most people on the East End didn't even know that two murders had occurred.

And now, I found myself wondering what the sheriff had really found on Eddie's computer, and if, in fact, there were some nutty, disappointed woman, who'd decided to murder him. Unfortunately, I didn't know enough people in town to settle on a likely candidate, but I would keep an open mind on that issue for sure.

It was a beautiful, clear day. One of those days that made you feel good to be alive. Things got quiet in the library around midday, the way they often did when the beach beckoned. I carried my tuna fish sandwich out to the bench in front where I could take in the view of the bay.

Ellen had the same idea, except she wasn't eating canned tuna like me, but a cupful of fresh strawberries. We sat side-by-side looking out over the shimmering sea in front of us.

The midday sun was still shining, but far out on the horizon we could see some dark clouds forming, and now and then a streak of lightning cut across them, like a golden ribbon on a gift.

Ellen reached for her purse. "I think we should go back inside. The way that storm is moving, I think it'll be here soon."

As the two of us got up from the bench, there was a loud clap of thunder.

Only it wasn't thunder.

It was one of the marble figures that decorated the posts on the widow's walk.

It exploded on the bench, splitting it in two and sending fragments of marble in all directions. Ellen and I both screamed. We'd been sitting there only seconds before, and surely would have been killed if we hadn't stood up at the moment we had.

As it was, a sliver of marble struck me in the knee and another one hit my shoulder. As Ellen and I looked at each other with mouths open, and Letitia Rose and a couple of others ran out of the library and down the steps toward us, the heavens opened, and the rain came down in torrents, soaking us all almost instantly.

Letitia Rose yelled over the squalling downpour, "Thank God you're all right. What a terrible, terrible accident!"

As she and Ellen ran back up the stairs toward cover, I stood there picking up a few more pieces of the shattered figure. Which is when I saw the metal identifying plate.

It was Humpty Dumpty who had almost killed my friend Ellen and me. I dashed up the steps after the rest, and as I did, I remembered the words of the grand dame of British mysteries, P.D. James, who said that, as a child, she wondered whether Humpty Dumpty had fallen off the wall or been pushed.

Inside, the library staff fussed over us, handing us towels from the supply closet so we could dry off. There were of course blessings to all the gods, from Neptune to Mary, Queen of Angels, giving thanks that the bolt of lightning that had separated the statue from its base, hadn't harmed us, and soon the usual group of mothers and children, as well as lonely senior citizens, returned to their browsing and reading, and Ellen and I returned to answering questions and stamping out books, as if nothing unusual had happened.

But the more I replayed the incident in my mind, the more convinced I became that it had not been an accident. I grabbed Ellen's hand and whispered in her ear. "That statue fell from the widow's walk *before* the lightning hit!"

Ellen shook her head. "I don't think so. I told you that storm was coming fast."

"I could still see it in the distance."

"Did you also see a ghost again?"

I had to admit I'd seen nothing but the rain after the initial crash of the statue. But I still didn't believe there was anything accidental about what had happened to us.

***

My knee and shoulder hurt where they'd been cut with the shards of splintered marble but what was really causing me pain was thinking about my future life in Pilgrim's Landing. Pilgrim's Landing? My future life anywhere!

It was possible the phony ghost I'd encountered was only trying to scare me to keep me from asking too many questions. But the fallen statue was meant to kill. Whether it was meant to kill me or Ellen—or both of us—was really the only open question.

On way home, as I rode my bike down Main Street, I passed Job's art shop. It was simply called The Olde Art Shoppe. Inside, I could see a tall figure in dark trousers and vest bending close to Job. That had to be Winston. Of course, they both worked at the library and were on town boards together but there was such a difference of age and attitude that I never thought of them as close.

Still, both had always been very kind to me. They were horrified by my most recent escape from tragedy and had showered me with special gifts. Winston had offered me a drink from his personal silver flask, and Job had sneaked me a candy bar I was not allowed to eat in the library.

It seemed only right for me to stop and say thanks and perhaps even sop up a little more sympathy for my lonely plight.

The light inside the shop allowed me to watch my two friends for a while, without their seeing me. It made me feel good to see Winston out of his "den" at the library and in what seemed like a fully sober state.

And Job, a lonely man, could use a friend who shared his interests, instead of simply hanging out with his drinking chums at Mohican's bar.

Winston held several papers in his hand, and he kept pointing to various portions of these papers, while Job either shook his head or nodded.

I knew well the feeling of loneliness. It washed over me now. I had never been inside Job's shop, and since Messi hadn't called, I had nothing but a dark, empty cottage waiting for me.

So, I parked my bike in the alleyway and opened the door to the shop.

A little bell rang when the door opened, and Winston spun away from Job as if he had received an electric shock.

Job also seemed disturbed, swinging around, the papers in his lap falling to the floor.

"Sorry! Didn't mean to scare you guys. "

I moved to help them pick up the papers, but Job quickly rolled his wheelchair on top of them, so I couldn't retrieve them.

"Don't bother about those. Just scribble sheets. I'll deal with them later. How nice to see you!"

In the meantime, Winston was busy shoving his half of the "scribble sheets" or whatever they were into a battered briefcase he usually had stashed close to him at the library.

I did the best I could to pretend I'd seen nothing unusual.

"I was passing by and saw the two of you through the window. So I decided to stop in to say hello, and also thank you for all your comforting words after the statue fell."

Winston, always the gentleman, seemed to recover first. "How thoughtful you are. A real asset to the library. You know, it takes a great deal to satisfy Letitia Rose, but you have managed to do it."

Job rolled his wheelchair off the papers on the floor until he could reach down and scoop them up. He tucked them into the pocket of a jacket hanging on a peg on the wall.

I looked around the shop, staring at a display of old cameras on one of the shelves.

"Can I help you?" Job asked.

"I guess I just wondered what you guys really thought of the sheriff. I can't help thinking that he's on the take and covering up for someone, or he's running some kind of scam. Why else blame it all so quickly on an innocent kid?"

"What kind of scam?" Job asked

"Maybe rare books or stolen documents. It's so dark and dreary on that lower floor, hardly anyone goes down there. The sheriff could be running a prostitution ring for all I know."

Winston winced. "Oh my. Letitia Rose would just die if something like that was happening in her library."

"And what about that stuff he claimed he found on Eddie's computer? Something 'too sensitive to discuss in front of women?' Do you think Eddie was involved in something... kinky? I don't want to give Bill Bronson another chance to blame the murders on an innocent person, but I don't want to close the door on the possibility that there could have been a jealous woman involved."

Winston really seemed shocked that I would even bring up such a subject, and just made some guttural sounds in his throat and turned away.

Job wheeled closer to me. "Do you have any proof of these things?"

"Not yet. I just have this...feeling. Especially about there being some kind of 'cover-up.' We all need to keep our eyes open."

I pointed to the shelf of old cameras. They were the sort I had only ever seen in my grandfather's house—large and boxy, with an accordion midsection and a black fabric cape. I'd once had my photo taken at an antiques fair with one. The photographer puts his head inside the fabric hood to help control the light that comes in. I remember being surprised at how good the photo actually turned out.

There were several other large cameras, the kind with big flashbulbs that Hawkeye still used.

"Do any of those cameras still work?" I asked.

Job rolled his wheelchair behind the counter and lifted one of the old box cameras up.

"I'm sure it would, but we can't get film for it anymore."

He lovingly wiped the lens with the edge of his T-shirt and replaced it on the shelf.

Then he picked up one of the cameras with the large flashbulb attachment.

"This guy? I used it to photograph a white whale that was washed up on Sands End."

He picked up a smaller camera in a tattered leather case. "This one? This one I got off a dead soldier in Afghanistan, right before his friend put a bullet in my back."

Winston shook his head. "Oh now, Job. Please let's not talk about such things. We have better things to show our friend. Now, come over here, my dear, and take a look at this wonderful early map of Pilgrim's Landing."

On the side wall was a large map crisscrossed with different colored lines and small blocks of color. Winston took my hand and traced a curving line from Pilgrim's Landing to Bliss Bay.

"That's an old Shinnecock Road. Goes all the way out there to Bliss Bay and even further—if you follow that small green line—out to Sands End."

When I got close, I could see that the blocks of color I was staring at were really buildings—beautifully drawn replicas of The First Olde Church, the windmill on the point near Bliss Bay, a line of small cottages rimming the ocean side of Pilgrim's Landing. There were blocks of green and yellow outlining corn and wheat fields. There were even small seagulls flying over the bay.

"How absolutely wonderful! Where did you get this? I've never seen anything like it anywhere!"

Winston smiled. "Actually, my dear, you have seen it, but you never really *looked* at it. There is a small version of this map right outside the ladies' room at the library.

"Yes! Yes! That's right—but under glass and small—I thought it was a fancy reproduction of something. But this—this is the original! Who made it? Where did it come from?"

Winston beamed, and now Job's mood seemed to lift as well.

He rolled over to the map. "It's my map. I made it, with a little help from a friend—Winston."

Even as we stood together staring at the map, Winston called out, "Oops! No. this will never do." And he walked over to one of the supply drawers and took out a small bottle of something with a strong smell of turpentine, and another small bottle of black ink. From another drawer, he fetched a pen, fit a point to it and walked back to the map.

"Right here, Job! This corner. It's wrong. That is where the old Halsey Tackle Shop used to be. You have it wrong." And right before my eyes, he dabbed a chemical on a small store front, blew on the canvas or parchment or whatever the material was and, after the image magically disappeared, gave the pen to Job.

Job shook his head. "Not now, Winston, I think this young lady would like to go home and eat her dinner. I need to look at a photo of the tackle shop before I can draw it. I can't just spit these things out."

Whatever tension I had created when I made my surprise appearance seemed to have totally dissipated now, as we all stared with admiration at the amazing map on the wall.

"You need to share this with everyone on the East End. You should have a special exhibition or something. It's too beautiful to keep hidden here in your store!"

Job shook his head. "The people who appreciate such things know where to find them. The others don't really count."

"I've been trying to convince him for years that giving the map to the library is the right thing to do, but thus far I have not been successful."

Winston took my arm and led me to the door. "Perhaps you can get him to change his mind."

I waved goodnight to Job, and Winston locked the door behind me.

As I climbed back on my bike, I could see them in the office, conferring closely again, though I couldn't hear what was being said.

And then I saw Job pull out the "scribble sheets" he had stashed in his jacket and lay them on the counter. I watched Winston retrieve the papers he had put in his briefcase and wave them in front of Job.

I peddled slowly home in the dark, wondering what the hell it was all about.

CHAPTER TEN

"He (Uncas) saved my life in the coolest and readiest manner and he has made a friend who never will require to be reminded of the debt he owes."

—James Fenimore Cooper, *The Last of the Mohicans*

I t was a beautiful evening and everyone at the library, at least, was trying to get back to normal life, whatever that might mean.

The sheriff had returned the knife to Letitia Rose; Jose had mysteriously been released by the sheriff's office without any notice from the rest of the community; and the library had returned to its usual hours and activities.

Messi, for his part, seemed to remember that we had shared some kind of intimate relationship and decided he wanted to see me again.

"Heard there was an accident at the library," he said. "One of those silly statues the town put up to try to impress everyone on the East End. Waste of money, if you ask me. Good thing you and Ellen had enough sense to come in out of the rain. Lightning travels faster than thunder in these parts."

I was still reluctant to tell Messi what I really thought about the so-called "accident," so I just nodded and said, "I can move even more quickly on land than in the water."

"No sailor could wish for more! I thought you might enjoy some whale and dolphin watching. Have you ever seen any close up?"

I clapped my hands like a little kid. What person who loves to swim hasn't dreamed of seeing these amazing creatures up close?

"Bring a change of clothes, a sweatshirt and long pants. It can get pretty windy offshore."

He sat in a chair in the kitchen while I gathered my clothes. "You can skip the bathing suit. It just gets in the way."

I handed him a canvas bag. "In the way of what?"

He pulled me close. "Nature."

We took the back roads, etched now in my memory from Job's map, many not more than Indian paths, worn down by more than a hundred years of tracking. We parked in the woods and went down to the bay, where the dingy was tied up.

And there was Hawkeye, untying the rope, handing Messi the oars and mumbling greetings to us both. We pushed off quietly and followed the rays of the sunset, out into open water.

"Hawkeye seems to adore both you and Hal. He follows Hal around all day, and you all night. When does he sleep?"

Messi dipped his oar rhythmically into the water. "Maybe he doesn't sleep. He's 'The Last of the Mohicans,' and has to watch his ass."

"Just so you know, Hawkeye is not the name of the Indian but the Indian name for his friend, the white hunter and trapper. The actual last of the Mohicans is named Chingachgook. He becomes the last of the Mohicans when his son Uncas is killed."

"Well now, Miss Librarian. That is a really interesting piece of information. I bet our Hawkeye is real happy no one named him Chingachgook. What can I tell you about the East End as a trade?"

"You can explain why Hawkeye follows Hal around like a puppy. I can understand his affection for you because you're Nature Boy incarnate, but what is going on with Hal?"

"Hawkeye is his grandson."

This revelation left me speechless, which prompted a great laugh from my friend Messi.

"You don't know everything, Miss Librarian. There are still quite a few things I can teach you. His son fell in love with a beautiful Indian maiden, and nobody was happy about it. Certainly not the Shinnecock. They're a very proud people. They were even more unhappy when the Indian maiden died in childbirth and her mate disappeared. Hal is one of those pilgrim people with the three names you talk about, and he did not want those names to disappear, so he did what he could for the boy."

I looked back at the shore, and I could see now that familiar splashing right below Messi's house. I knew that Hawkeye was involved in it, somehow, some way.

"He may pay the kid a salary, but he hasn't acknowledged the kid as his own. That must suck."

Messi laughed again. He was really enjoying my ignorance this evening.

"Sorry to have to tell you but you don't have a clue about what you are saying. People here have attitudes going back to Columbus. The most you can expect from them is that they act in some kind of human way to blood relatives—even if they're ashamed to acknowledge the connection. As for Hawkeye—he knows that many of these pilgrims have the same feelings of love and desire and respect for excellence everyone has. No one here would ever think of Hawkeye as a 'half-breed.' He has a combination of Indian skills and white-man skills that are impressive to the entire community."

"So, he's happy as a clam."

"Maybe he is. And speaking of clams, you owe me."

I decided it was time to shut up. I peered silently into the sunset until we reached the boat.

Messi tied up the dingy and this time, I scampered aboard the fishing boat like an old salt. I was getting stronger and more seaworthy by the minute. Messi stashed my clothes below deck and started up the motor.

We headed out into open water, skimming across the waves.

It seemed to me that only a few minutes later I heard Messi shouting, "There! There!" and pointing straight ahead. Three or four dolphins were frolicking, jumping and diving in and out of the water, sending geysers of water up into the air and making a racket of clicking sounds.

Messi cut the motor and we floated nearby. Three of the four took off so fast I could hardly see them they got so far away in just seconds. One kept circling and circling and making clicking sounds. He looked really big up close, with one flipper that was almost all white.

Messi looked over the side and started making clicking noises of his own. "He's looking for food. "

I tried to remember if I had stashed a candy bar somewhere while Messi grabbed a large can of what smelled like odds and ends of various disgusting fish from the bin at the stern.

The clicking sounds grew louder.

"I think he smells the food," Messi said, dumping the can overboard.

In an instant, all the chunks of fish and bones were gone, and the dolphin was circling and clicking again.

And then he bumped the boat.

We tilted to one side and for a moment I thought I was going overboard, but Messi held me tight with one hand while steering with the other.

"These dolphins are friendly, but they're curious," he said. "And they don't understand that we don't play the same way they play. I think we'd better go." He started the engine, and we motored away, the sky now a deep purple. When he deemed us sufficiently far away, he cut the engine and lowered the anchor. Then he moved to the back of the boat and sat down next to me.

"Time for a swim." He lifted off my t-shirt and unhooked my bra. "I don't know why you wear all this unnecessary clothing. It feels so much nicer to swim when you're naked. No one to see you out here except me and the dolphins."

I pulled off the rest of my clothing, and we dove into the moonlit waters of the bay. Messi moved gracefully, slowly cutting through the water, then circling back to me. It was like a sweet replay of that other night, except that as we came together in an embrace, I happened to look over his shoulder at the spot where we'd left the boat...and there was no boat! It was gone!

"The boat!" I gasped, pointing in the direction it had been.

Messi turned, scanning the empty horizon. In a stern and commanding voice, he said, "Stay here. I'll come back for you in a minute!"

And then he was gone.

I called out to him, but there was no answer.

But I listened to his orders and stayed where I was. After a while, I got tired of treading water. I spread out my arms and legs and leaned back, floating to save energy. I knew there were sharks in these waters. I wondered if I should kick my feet to scare them away, or if that might do the opposite and attract them instead. I wanted desperately to go after Messi, but I suddenly realized I no longer had any idea which way to swim.

The moon that had shined so brightly just a few minutes ago had disappeared behind the clouds.

The stars—also gone.

The twinkling lights that lined the shore, gone.

It was so dark I could barely see my hand in front of my face. Completely quiet except for the waves splashing against my chest.

How would Messi find me?

Even Neptune wouldn't be able to find me now!

Things can so quickly turn deadly in the water. I had never felt so alone. No lifeguards, no family waiting for me on shore. No subway to bring me back to where I started from.

People say that when you're dying—or think you are going to die—your whole life flashes in front of you. I thought of the husband I had left, and the comfort of a big, warm apartment on Fifth Avenue. I thought of my mother, who worried when I swam out too far at Rockaway Beach. And I thought of my blue baby—kicking her little feet, her tiny face scrunched up, her mouth gasping for air.

And then I thought of Marna van Dugan—Messi's last girlfriend who had mysteriously drowned at sea. It could have happened just like this. Abandoned in the middle of the ocean. Not knowing which direction to swim, the night dark, rain coming down.

Was Messi a murderer, or just someone who attracted bad luck? Was he Neptune or Satan, or just an ignorant sailor who thought he could do more than he really could?

And then the terrible words of King Lear washed over me with the force of a tsunami.

"As flies to wanton boys are we to the gods. They kill us for their sport."

Was that what I was to Messi? A new sport?

And then, as the cloud cover shifted slightly, I saw a white fin cut the water a few feet away from me and slowly circle closer.

My breath caught in my throat, as if I had already exited my life. Which is when I heard the unmistakable clicking noise of a dolphin.

It circled around me, clicking and clicking. Was it the one we had fed from the boat? I tried to swim toward it until—yes!—I saw that strange white flipper!

All I know was it didn't bump me. It came close enough for me to look into its eye, but it didn't bump me.

What it did was make a more urgent trilling sound while I watched it and tread water. Then it turned around and made almost a monkey sound, wagging it's snout.

Was it flirting with me? Inviting me to play?

What else could it mean? Was this giant fish trying to tell me to follow it? How could that be possible? Messi had told me not to move, that he would come back to get me. If I followed the dolphin, Messi might never find me. But as I stared into the dark and silent sea, wondering what I should do, I heard the motor of the boat and a different clicking sound altogether.

The lights were on in the boat. I saw Messi at the wheel, clicking for all he was worth.

The huge creature turned and headed for the boat, and I saw Messi throw out something white and shiny. He cut the motor and dove in beside me.

He was holding his knife in his teeth and when he rose to the surface, his long hair flowing around him, all I could think of was that he was not Neptune; he was not Satan; he was Tarzan of the sea.

In a flash, Messi lifted me onto the ladder and turned to meet the dolphin, who had circled back again.

Again, Messi made loud clicking sounds and threw something white and shiny way out to sea. Then he clambered up after me, started the motor and we took off like meteorites into the night.

I lay on the deck, trying to catch my breath, my entire body trembling. Messi kept reassuring me from the wheel, "You'll be okay. I promise. You'll be okay. Breathe. Just breathe."

At that moment, I began to cry. Great, wracking sobs that shook me to my core. I'm not a crier. The last time I'd cried, in fact, had been when I'd seen my blue baby. But now it spilled out of me in great heaving jerks.

Messi dropped anchor and came over and hugged me. Then he brought my clothes up from the hold and gently helped me dress while I cried and cried until at last, I couldn't cry anymore, and my breathing, though still jagged, began to calm.

He once again disappeared down below again, this time coming back with a silver flask. "It's scotch. I know you only like vodka, but it's all I have. It'll make you feel better. I promise."

He took a long swallow himself first and then offered it to me. "Better than a raw clam."

It didn't require eating a raw clam to know that.

#####

Breathing normally again, I unwound myself from Messi's arms and allowed reason to once more return to my brain as I tried to make sense of the whole experience, asking him what had just happened and how. Messi explained that for some reason, the anchor hadn't held, and once the boat got caught up in the current, it drifted away quickly.

That I could understand. But it was the dolphin that really confused me. Could Messi talk to dolphins? I wasn't a superstitious person but some of the interactions between Messi and the sea were downright weird.

"Were you talking to that dolphin?"

"It's cool that you think I have supernatural powers, but the truth is there are tapes of dolphin noises like there are tapes of bird calls. Human beings can imitate the sounds to get their attention. It's great when you take tourists out whale watching. I know where they hang out and I even have a special friend—that big one with the white flipper. He comes around for chopped up pieces of fish occasionally, and he loves to play. I have a couple of white tennis balls that some rich dude left on the boat, so I threw them out as a diversion. I didn't want to take any chances with that big dolphin trying to make you its playmate."

"So, what are you? A fish whisperer? Tarzan of the Sea?"

"For one thing, Miss Librarian, dolphins are not fish. They're sea mammals. And yes, there are some that I talk to. So, if that makes me Tarzan of the Sea, does that make you Jane?"

The only thing I remembered about Jane was her ability to climb trees and ride an elephant while holding on to Boy. The only thing the two of us had in common was some athletic ability and the adventurousness to negotiate a dangerous landscape. But she had succeeded in producing Boy while I had only a blue baby struggling to escape the suffocating folds of my memory.

We headed back to Messi's mooring, tied up, and rowed the dingy to shore, once again confronted by the splashing and murmuring of a dozen shadowy figures digging in the shallow water. Just a short time before, all I'd been thinking about was staying alive, but now my curiosity had returned. I had questions.

"Will you please tell me what in hell is going on here?"

He looked at me, as enigmatic as ever.

"Whatever it is, Messi, I'm not gonna turn you in. For Chrissakes, you just saved my life. Can't you trust me, just a little?"

I didn't know whether he felt sorry for me or guilty, but after he helped me out of the dingy, he walked back out into the shallow water and dug into the sand. I half-expected him to come up with a hated, dreaded clam. Instead, he unfurled his hand to reveal a large oyster.

He took out his knife and opened the shell. Then he held it out, so the moon, which was shining brightly once more, lit the inside. There, in the center of the fleshy glob, was a gray-white pearl.

Messi flicked his knife and dislodged the pearl into my hand.

"It's the Indians oyster bed. They're experts at seeding oysters. They plant a tiny irritant—a piece of clam shell, a piece of fish bone—I'm not really privy to all their secrets, but after they put them back in the water, eventually a pearl forms. Their tribe has been seeding oysters like this for generations. Still, you can't own a part of the ocean floor, so we try to keep it a secret."

I rolled the pearl around the palm of my hand. "It's so amazing. It's so beautiful, like a piece of a star."

"Keep it. It's a gift—a good-luck charm." He looked in my eyes. I tried to divine the feelings behind his gaze, but there was still so much mystery there, I wasn't sure what to think.

"I think we should get out of here," he said, taking my hand and guiding me up the path to the woods where he'd parked his car. Then he drove me home.

***

Strangely, though perhaps not too strangely, I felt safer in the library than I did in the water, even with a murderer on the loose. At least here in the library I was surrounded by people. As long as I didn't stay alone at night after closing time, I figured I'd be okay. After all, I'd survived living in New York City all these years.

The big news at the library is that we'd closed entries for submission to the photo contest that Letitia Rose and the *Pilgrim's Landing Star* were sponsoring. People had responded, and there were plenty of entries. The only restriction was that the photos submitted feature local scenes, photos taken somewhere on the East End—from Pilgrim's Landing to Bliss Bay and Sands End. Each entry needed to include a title, identify the location of the scene photographed, and list the name and age of the participant.

I was excited to be able to choose, along with Ellen and Job, which qualifying photos to put on display. Of course, Letitia Rose watched over us like a hawk.

"We're a community library. We have a mission," she lectured us. "That means that we should try to represent everyone who took the time to submit a photo—even if it doesn't exactly meet our artistic expectations."

In real terms, that meant that we had to include the blurry photo of "My cat, Stinky, sitting on my porch swing," by Mandy Potter age 7, Bliss Bay; as well as "My friends, Sandy, Kathy and Donna, in my Red Bentley, overlooking Bliss Bay," by Patrick McDuffy Heinz, 23, Pilgrim's Landing."

There were entries from Henry Long-Bow Norton, and Tiffany Johnson, Jerzy Polansky and Jesus Torres. Winston submitted a photo of his home "Angels Rest," perched high on the cliff at Heaven's Edge, overlooking the ocean at Pilgrim's Landing.

In the end, we found room for just about every photo except for a couple, submitted anonymously, of someone sitting on a toilet bowl, and another featuring an erect penis.

Actually, I was sorry we hadn't posted these, because they were among the most original. Most of the rest just featured pretty gardens, a brightly colored beach umbrella against the white sand beach, and a bunch of tanned children playing in the surf.

But Job did not share my jaundiced view. "Look at the depth and sense of movement in this photo of a bunch of marigolds. Look at the unusual angle of this shot off the top of the cliff at Conscience Crossing. Look at this shot through the water of the pebbles on the water's edge."

The one thing missing was the supposedly "stunning" photo taken by Messi that would humiliate, terrify, and ultimately render Sheriff Bill Bronson harmless. Where was it?

It was Job who found it. "Take a look at this photo of a local police car —the angle—from above—the deliberate blurring of the object on the ground. The whole scene suggests something eerie, mysterious. Even the title, 'Hit and Run,' photographed on Route 27, Sands End."

I looked more closely at the photo. The photographer was listed as Issem King.

"Issem King. Issem King. Sounds Arabic. Are there any Arabic families on the East End?"

Job laughed. "Are you kidding? They still don't like to rent to Hispanics. Must be some visitor staying at one of the motels in the area."

And then, suddenly, I got it. "Issem" was Messi spelled backwards.

I looked more carefully at the photo. There was a clear date on the lower right corner, the kind of date that some digital cameras imprint on the image. The police car was turned at an angle on the road and under the wheels was a dark, indistinct shape. The lighting was dim, mostly coming from a full moon overhead.

I wasn't sure what this photo might mean to the sheriff, but it didn't mean much to me. At any rate, I didn't want to spend too much time looking at it or get Job all worked up about something he might or might not be privy to, and so I turned my attention to another photo in the pile—a young man holding up a large fish he had just caught.

The tag read: "Josh Martin, age 23, Largemouth Bass, caught 8/16/18, Lake Minnehaha, Pilgrim's Landing."

"The kid caught that fish in a lake. Messi would really be jealous!"

"Messi has nothing to be jealous about when it comes to fish. He could fill a photo album with the tuna he catches every summer. And lakes are not really his venue—much too tame. Are you still going out with him?"

I nodded.

"I like Messi. Very unusual guy. But there's something... something hidden, something mysterious about him. He lives here, but he's really not one of us. He plays by his own rules. And you know what happened to his last girlfriend."

I shook my head. "No—I really don't know what happened to her. Do you think he murdered her? Does everyone in town believe he murdered her?"

"I can't speak for everyone. She was pregnant with someone else's child. "

So that's why he wouldn't marry her!

"Whose child? Who do people say was the father?"

"He was an addict. He died from an overdose."

Ellen saw us whispering and moved in. "It's all just rumors. The girl was a junkie herself."

I looked from Job to Ellen and back again but before I could learn anything more, Letitia Rose broke up our little group.

"You all need to get working. Tomorrow is our opening. I see a whole stack of photos not even framed yet, much less put on the wall!"

So, we all got to work again, with no chance the rest of the day to continue our conversation. We used colored tape that peeled off easily to frame each photo and we used double-sided tape so as not to mar the walls of the library's main floor.

Giovanni's Deli donated some chips and dip; Sojourner Truth Spirits donated wine and fizzy water, and we all prepared to do our town, and its townsfolk, proud.

***

The sheriff didn't come to the opening, but his deputy did, along with almost everyone in town. It helped that it was a rainy day and there was free food. Of course, the widow Sally Brier Montgomery was there, spearing pieces of salami with a plastic toothpick; the coroner came with his wife and daughter; Hal was there peering at all the photos and sipping some wine; there were clusters of tanned young people from Bliss Bay, decked out with Prada purses and Gucci shoes; and even an assortment of small children, taking handfuls of potato chips.

I was pleased to see a large number of Mexican families show up. Many of the Hispanic kids in the area spent a good deal of time in the library, and we offered English classes to their parents. But since recent government threats to deport every brown person without the proper papers, many of the usual visitors to the library stayed home. Today, though, I was able to happily greet Maria Gonzalez, Israel Vargas, Rosa Casita, and many other regulars. Even Jose Lopez had shown up. He nodded at me before approaching the snack table.

The Shinnecock were sure enough of their citizenship to show up as well. Hawkeye and a couple of elderly Indians, their tanned skin etched with fine lines that would have done any photographer proud, peered with great curiosity at the prints on the wall.

The long established African American group appeared as well, and I felt proud of my adopted town, a mix of so many colors, ages and styles of dress. Even Manhattan would have difficulty matching this ethnic stew of people and personalities.

And there was the sheriff's deputy with the squashed-in nose, staring at the photo of the police car with its caption, "Hit and Run." I walked up to him. "Interesting photo, don't you think?"

He forced a smile, then walked off, looking somewhat rattled. I went over to the snack table and speared a piece of salami with a toothpick.

That's when I saw Messi. He walked over to the deputy and said something to him. I moved closer, so I could hear them, but all I caught was Messi saying, "Please give my regards to the sheriff," right before the deputy turned on his heel and walked off. When Messi saw me, he just nodded, as if we were mere acquaintances, and made his to the other side of the room.

I found Ellen and tried to get some information from her about the Marna Von Dugan situation, as well as the deputy, but Ellen just mumbled something about nasty rumors, and said she didn't have any intel on the deputy.

"Do you know anything? Where's he from? What's his relationship with the sheriff?"

"All I know is he showed up here two, maybe three years ago. A poor kid. Used to box over there at Sands End where they bet on stuff like that. Got knocked around. Sheriff gave him a job. He mostly does the heavy lifting for Bill Bronson—breaking down doors, carrying body bags, that sort of thing. With all the bad stuff the sheriff is into, he probably also needs a personal bodyguard."

"Messi will be disappointed. He put up that photo just to scare the sheriff."

"You worry too much about Messi. He can take care of himself."

Letitia Rose, who managed to be everywhere at once, now stood in front of the food and wine table and rang a little bell.

The sound was so unexpected in a library that it reduced all of us to silence.

"Thank you one and all for coming to our summer photo exhibition. We hope you learned more about each other and the beautiful East End. Now, while all of you deserve admiration for your work, there are a few photos that our experts—Job, our art director and teacher—in consultation with other members of the library staff, believes deserve special recognition."

Letitia Rose motioned to Job, and he stood next to her. "First Prize goes to Josh Martin and the beautiful fish he caught in our very own Lake Minnehaha!"

A cheer went up, and a young man of about 16 came up to the table. Job pinned a red ribbon on his shirt.

"Can you tell us something about how you caught the fish and how you managed to take a selfie while holding it up like that?"

"I was just casting around, and all of a sudden I felt a tug on the line. I thought it was a turtle, but when I reeled it in, it turned out to be a largemouth bass. My mom said I couldn't keep it—it was just for sport—so she handed me the camera and I snapped the shot."

There were more cheers and applause and Josh walked back to the wall and stood next to his photo while Hawkeye snapped his photo for the *Pilgrim's Landing Star*.

"Second prize goes to something entirely different—an eerie, mysterious photo shot in the early evening: Issem King, age 55, from Sands End."

There was some applause and then a great shuffling around as everyone turned this way and that to see the prize winner come forward.

"Issem? Issem King?" Job called out again. "Well, let's have a round of applause for Issem, who seems not to have been able to attend this evening. If anyone here knows Issem, please let him know he can pick up his second-prize blue ribbon at the library front desk."

I watched Messi, who looked innocently this way and that. I watched him clap his hands with enthusiasm along with the rest of the crowd. Afterwards, I watched him move easily from one group of people to the next, shaking hands, squeezing shoulders. What did he have on the sheriff and what did the sheriff have on him?

One thing seemed sure: I was not going to get any answers to my questions any time soon.

***

The next morning was bright and cool. I dressed quickly in my black trousers and white shirt, eager to get to the library and find out if there were any new developments connected to the photo exhibition.

I grabbed my bike helmet, jumped on my bike, and started down the steep path to the highway when the front wheel started buckling. I tried to drag my feet to stop the bike from moving but it was going too fast. A branch from one of the scraggly birches that lined the property hit me in the chest, and while I hung on to the handlebars, the front wheel spun off the frame of the bike, which flipped and sent me crashing into and bouncing off the trunk of a large oak tree.

I lay there for a few minutes, while I summoned the courage to see if I could move my arm.

My shirt was covered with dirt and torn at the elbow, and when I straightened my arm, I felt a throbbing ache and blood ran down the sleeve. Bruised—but not, it seemed, broken.

My legs seemed to move okay too, except my pants were torn at the knee and there was a little blood showing through there, too.

Luckily, I was wearing my helmet and, as I lay on the soft ground, I gave thanks that something— perhaps Pepe's little silver cross or Messi's pearl—had protected me yet again.

Finally, steady enough to get up and gather the pieces of my bike, I received another shock: the lug nuts that held the front wheel tight in the frame were missing!

I'm a city girl, born and bred. Perhaps that's why I've never much liked to drive. Sure, I have a driver's license. Like learning to swim, it's something my parents insisted I learn when I turned 18. But I always felt more comfortable on a bike than in the driver's seat of a car. I didn't know how to change a tire on a car, but I knew how to check a tire on a bike, and I checked the screws and the air pressure on the front and back tires regularly.

Someone had deliberately sabotaged my bike in the hope that I would have a fatal accident.

Or perhaps, they didn't count on a fatal accident. Just a few broken bones to keep me from looking too closely into affairs that were none of my business.

Whatever the motive, I was sure that this—like the fallen statue of Humpty Dumpty—was no accident. I would have to change my clothes and wash my face (which I now discovered was dripping a little blood, too), before I showed up at the library.

I limped slowly back up to the cottage and called Messi.

***

"Tell me again what you said to Job and Winston when you surprised them in Job's store."

I sat at my kitchen table and Messi paced the floor. "I told them that I suspected the sheriff was covering for someone. That... that... that someone at the library was doing something illegal and he was covering for them."

Messi plopped down on the chair next to me. "And it never occurred to you that one of them—if not both of them—was involved in these illegal activities?"

"I never thought...I thought they were my friends."

"Well, wake up, Little Suzie. You're not in Kansas anymore."

"The name of the girl in *The Wizard of Oz*...."

"Oh, shut up!" Messi said, and he kissed me gently on my bruised lips.

I sat at the table holding an ice pack to my cheek, wondering if it was the bruise causing me pain or just the fact that I was grinding my teeth.

Messi put his arms around me. "There's no sense beating yourself up over this. The truth is we're probably one step closer to finding Eddie's murderer and probably Pepe's as well. It may have been one—or even both of them—or someone they hired to do the dirty work. The problem is what to do now. We need some real proof. This is murder. You're in the line of fire, and whoever it is, isn't kidding around."

"So what do we do?"

"I need to consult with some friends. But first, I'm gonna give you a lift to the library. You just tell everyone you fell off your bike. And don't go anywhere alone until we meet up again. Got it?"

I got that I was in danger. I got that Messi was going to help me. What I didn't get was how he was going to do it.

CHAPTER ELEVEN

"Better to sleep with a sober cannibal than a drunk Christian."

—**Herman Melville**, *Moby Dick*

"Now Lettie, I'll thank you to please take down that photo with the police car. This is the U.S. of A., and we don't need any A-rabs posting photos that say bad things about police activities in Pilgrim's Landing."

Apparently, the sheriff's deputy had let the sheriff know about the prize-winning photo by Issem King. The law was not happy.

And neither was Letitia Rose.

"Bill Bronson, you know we had a photo exhibition here at our library and this young man won a prize fair and square. Isn't anyone going to think bad things about our police 'cause a car appears in a photo. Isn't hardly anyone even reads the caption. What does it mean 'Hit and run' anyways? Looks to me like the police are after someone maybe broke the law of the land."

Bill Bronson took a knife out of his pocket and approached the photo. He obviously did not understand that we had stuck the photos on the wall with double-faced utility tape.

Letitia Rose put her hands on her hips. "Is that a weapon I see there in your hands, Bill Bronson? Are you threatening me with bodily harm?"

She turned to the front desk where Ellen and I were dutifully answering the phones.

"Miss Nussbaum and Miss Hinkley—do you see this man threatening my life? I do believe that is a felony of some sort."

The sheriff stepped away from the photo, but he did not put away his knife.

"Come on, Lettie! This Issem person is a threat to the entire community. And you give him a prize! Does anyone know who he is? I have looked through all the town records and I can find nobody with that name on the entire East End of Long Island. He is clearly some kind of terrorist. I have asked you nicely to take down that photo. If you do not, I may have to arrest you for obstructing justice. That photo is against the law."

"What law are you talking about? There is no law I can think of against a library posting a picture on a wall."

She held out her wrists to the sheriff. "Go ahead, arrest me. See if you can find a jury in Pilgrim's Landing to pronounce me guilty!"

"I'm in charge of law and order in this town, and I say that photo comes down."

"And I'm in charge of law and order in this library, and I say the photo stays exactly where it is!"

I knew that Letitia Rose was a strong and formidable character, but seeing her in action actually gave me a thrill. It was very gratifying to know that some people in town had no need to kiss the sheriff's ring. I was glad too that it was a little after five o'clock and the library was officially closed so there were no other witnesses to this encounter. None of us wanted a civil war in the village. I was just about to tell the sheriff that I thought this Issem person was a friend of Messi's when there was a loud knocking at the door.

I could see through the glass panes that it was Messi himself, and I moved quickly to open the doors, just as the sheriff yelled out, "Don't you dare let anyone in!"

I unlocked the door and, as Messi entered, shouted, "Oops!"

Messi looked from me to the sheriff, to Letitia Rose and back again. We all stood silent and frozen in place, as if someone had just stopped running a film.

"What seems to be the trouble?" Messi asked.

The sheriff pointed to the photo on the wall with the open blade of his knife.

"Son-of-a-bitch Moslem A-rab posts a photo of my police car and calls it 'Hit & Run.' Some terrorist tries to undermine the security of our town and this lady will not take it down."

Messi smiled. "Oh, is that all? This Issem character isn't a terrorist at all. He's a friend of mine."

"Since when are you friends with Moslems? Always thought you were a Catholic boy."

"Well, now. Bill Bronson. It's like this. Ever read *Moby Dick*? There's a dude there, name of Ishmael. Another dude, Queequeg, a dark-skinned person full of tattoos who throws a mean harpoon, might even be a cannibal. Me—I'm a fisherman. All kinds of people you never even heard of work on fishing boats. I don't ask whether they're going to heaven or hell, whether they pray to Neptune or Jesus or Mohammad—or not at all. Only thing matters to me is if they can gut a fish and reel in a line."

Messi stepped closer to the sheriff. "All my friend wants is to protect his friends. He heard there were a couple of murders right here in the library. He also told me he has some kind of 'evidence' 'bout some kind of ring or something going on. Doesn't want to embarrass anyone, and he isn't looking for any trouble. Knows me and you go way back. Just wants me to tell you that you need to be sure nothing else happens to anyone else here at the library—especially the librarian and the two assistant librarians—Miss Ellen Hinkley and Miss Sandra Nussbaum."

Messi walked over to the front desk and pointed at me.

"Looks like Miss Nussbaum here already had some kind of small accident with her bike. My friend, Issem King, he just wants your assurance that no other such accidents will happen to his friends. If you make sure of that, he will take care that his evidence does not fall into the wrong hands."

I watched in awe as this little scene played out before my eyes. I would say about halfway through this speech, the sheriff finally realized that Issem was

Messi. The color slowly drained from his face. His hand trembled, and he dropped the open knife on the floor.

In an instant, Messi had stepped on the knife so the sheriff couldn't pick it up. The two men came face to face. "Deal?" Messi asked.

The sheriff nodded.

Messi removed his foot from the knife on the ground.

"In that case, I really do think that my friend Issem would be willing to have his photo removed from the wall. As I said, he really isn't looking for trouble. Just safety and security."

At which point, Messi reached up, pulled the photo from the wall and handed it to the sheriff.

Then he turned to us, took off his baseball cap (it featured a diving dolphin and the words *Sands End*), bowed, and exited.

The sheriff turned to me. "Miss Nussheim, you stay away from that guy. He's bad news."

"It's Nuss*baum*."

"That's what I said." He mumbled something that sounded like "Issem King, my ass" and then he, too, left the library.

Letitia Rose sat down at the long oak reading table and breathed a sigh. Then she pulled me down next to her.

"I haven't forgotten about what you said about some forgery nonsense going on in my library. Are you saying a staff member of my library has been forging documents? I have known Job and Winston and even poor Eddie all their lives. Yes, Winston has a drinking problem, and Job, he can get depressed, and Eddie—he lived in the fog of his computer world—but forgery! Murder! That cannot be!"

I didn't want to burst her bubble of trust, but she needed to open her eyes.

"You have a whole room filed with valuable papers and documents from the old library that you've never taken out of cartons. You have shelves and shelves of books dating back to the 1800s. Nobody would know anything was missing unless a scholar came looking for a particular document or book."

I told her about the papers Ellen had showed me. I told her about the bottle of ink I'd found in Eddie's office, his stained fingers.

"All of them! You think they were all in it together? But why? Job has plenty of money. His family owns dozens of acres of land all over the East End. And Eddie—his family has millions of dollars, too. It's true that Winston doesn't have money and his father was a gambler, but he's an old man now. How much money does he need?"

Need? Everyone's needs are different. Right now, I had a need to wake Letitia Rose to a situation that had already taken two lives and might take more.

"I had a cousin who grew up poor and made millions, but he never moved from his little apartment in Manhattan. When I asked him why he lived like that when he was such a rich man, he told me he was not a rich man; he was a poor man with money. Here in Pilgrim's Landing, there are rich men without money. Why do rich men with money work at all? I think it's because they have a need to accomplish something on their own. They work because they enjoy working. Isn't that one of the Puritan values? Work is its own reward."

Letitia Rose nodded. "Amen! You got that right! Part of why I hired you!"

She pulled herself to her feet then and walked over to the "T" shelf. She ran her hands over the bindings of the books and then took out a copy of Huckleberry Finn. She flipped it open. "Here's Huck having second thoughts about the letter he wrote turning Jim in:

'I took it up and held it in my hand. I was a-trembling, because I'd got to decide, forever, betwixt two things, and I knowed it. I studied a minute, sort of holding my breath, and then says to myself:

'All right, then, I'll GO to hell'—and tore it up."

She carefully replaced the book and walked over to the "H" shelf. There, she had found a copy of Nathaniel Hawthorne's *The Scarlet Letter*.

"'Hold thy peace, dear little Pearl!'" whispered her mother. "We must not always talk in the marketplace of what happens to us in the forest.'"

She walked a little further down that row and pulled out a copy of Hemingway's *Old Man and the Sea*.

"'Now is no time to think of what you do not have. Think of what you can do with that there is.'"

And then, flipping a few more pages, she read: "'I may not be as strong as I think, but I know many tricks and I have resolution.'"

She put the book back in its place, and went to the "W" Shelf, where she quickly found a copy of Walt Whitman's *Leaves of Grass*.

"'Do I contradict myself? Very well, then I contradict myself, I am large, I contain multitudes.'"

She replaced the book and continued towards the beginning of the alphabet. At last, she stopped at the "C" shelf and took down a copy of *The Last of the Mohicans*.

"'Your young white, who gathers his learning from books and can measure what he knows by the page, may concede that his knowledge, like his legs, outruns that of his fathers, but where experience is the master, the scholar is made to know the value of years, and respects them accordingly.'"

She carefully replaced the book and returned to the long reading table.

"You're not the only one who stayed after hours in the library. I read the Bible to learn God's truth, but I read the books on these shelves to learn the truth of the human heart. These books are my children, and I used to visit them every night and kiss them—yes—kiss them good night. But that was many years ago."

She ran her hand over the smooth surface of the golden oak reading table.

"Love. After a while, you take it for granted. You carry it in your heart, and you no longer see what's right in front of your face."

She reached for my hand and looked me straight in the eye. Then she ran her hand gently over the bruise under my eye. "I will do whatever is necessary to protect my children!"

***

Messi knocked on my door the following evening. He pulled me outside and pointed to the sky, which was just beginning to get dark.

"See that, that's Jupiter up there. Over there is Mars. In the lighthouse at Sands End, they have a telescope that can show you the surface of the moon."

"What does it look like?"

"Rather boring, if you ask me. Lots of circles and rings. I'm just thinking up things to seduce you to spend the evening with me. Actually, the lighthouse closes to the public at five so how about I show you how to paddle a canoe?"

I had been so thoroughly seduced already by every aspect of Messi's personality that any extra props were certainly unnecessary, but hey, if he wanted to think he needed more bait to reel me in, that was okay with me. I brought along a sweatshirt and a pair of jeans this time, a change of underwear and my toothbrush, just in case he invited me to sleep over.

"It's a good thing you showed up when you did at the library," I said, as he started up his car. "The sheriff was about to arrest Letitia Rose for obstructing justice."

"In any contest between Bill Bronson and Letitia Rose, I'd put my money on Letitia Rose. How's your elbow and knee feeling? I can see your face is still a bit of a mess."

"Thanks a lot," I said, feigning offense.

"I mean, comely as hell despite that," he offered.

I laughed. "I've had worse knocks in my life. I'm glad your scheme to intimidate Bill Bronson worked, though. I thought he was going to have a heart attack when he finally realized it was you who had submitted that photo."

"That conversation between me and the sheriff was a long time coming. Hope he holds to his end of the bargain. Do not want to spend my days—and especially my evenings thinking about him. Survival on the East End of Long Island depends more on learning to paddle a canoe than head-butting with the likes of Bill Bronson."

Messi put the car in gear, and we headed for Sands End.

I thought I knew how to paddle a canoe, but I didn't want to spoil his fun. So, we drove along the water's edge all the way to Sands Point, with Messi pointing out this scenic rock and that sloping cliff until we arrived once again at the oyster farm beneath his cottage on the cliff.

Hawkeye greeted us with a big smile. "Heard my photo won the blue ribbon."

"Your photo! I thought it was taken by this Muslim kid, Issem. "

We all laughed, and I told him it was a beautiful photo and it had won fair and square because Job had no idea who had taken it. I was sorry he would not be able to show off his blue ribbon, but he just shrugged. He seemed to be used to letting others take the credit for what he had done.

We pushed off in the dingy, and Messi handed me a paddle.

"This is not a canoe. I don't know much about sea-going vessels, but I can tell a dingy from a canoe."

Messi rhythmically dipped his paddle into the water, first on one side and then the other.

"This dingy is much more stable than a canoe. 'Course the Indians know how to negotiate the waves, but for us white people, a dingy will do fine. Now, do you have a driver's license?"

"Yes. Of course."

"How often did you drive a car in New York City?"

I had to admit, very little. And the last time I had, I'd almost killed myself.

"So why did you get a driver's license?"

"Life insurance. My mom thought I should know how to drive in case my boyfriends were too drunk to drive me home."

"Right. So, out here, the equivalent is that you need to know how to row a canoe, or dingy, or whatever, maybe even a raft, like in Huckleberry Finn, because you never know when you might be called upon to use that skill."

He stood up in the dingy, which rocked side to side, nearly capsizing.

"See what I mean? You never know when you'll need a paddle. A paddle can be as good as a life jacket. If I had a paddle, instead of just a couple of rubber boots, I would have been rescued in two days instead of four."

Messi rarely talked about his close encounter with death. But other East End people still did. I decided it was a good thing to learn to paddle a canoe—or whatever.

Messi took my hand and placed it on the knobby heart-shaped handle. He put his hand over mine, and together we paddled the dingy out into the sea.

I leaned back against him, the strong muscles of his chest hard against my back. As we glided almost effortlessly through the water, Messi pointed out the fish swimming alongside us. "Look at that bluefish—over there—no—look at the ripples in the water going the other way—there! There! Follow the gulls—see that one dive! There's a school of bass out there! See that shadow in the water—there's something big out there—moving fast—shark after something." Messi could read the surface of the sea with the same ease I could read Shakespeare.

He took his hand off mine and let me paddle on my own. "When you want to turn, just back paddle—or switch the paddle to the other side. That's the way. Careful now. Don't go too fast or you can tip us over. That's fine."

We drifted along like that for 30 minutes or so until Messi asked, "Are you hungry?"

"That depends on what you're going to offer me. If it's a raw clam, forget it."

Messi smiled. "I have something you'll like much better."

He took over the paddling, and we soon came to his boat. When we climbed aboard, he opened the hatch to the cabin, and helped me down the ladder.

"Now, you sit right here." He pointed to a small table in the galley with a porthole looking out to sea.

He poured me a glass of wine, found an apron hung on a peg in the corner, and within minutes, I heard a happy humming sound and a *chop, chop* noise one of his chef's knives made slicing up vegetables on the cutting board.

From what I could see there were carrots and celery. Not bad so far.

Then he removed a large pot, took some liquid out of the refrigerator, and poured it in with the carrots and celery. He cut up an onion. My eyes began to tear.

Soon, the pungent smell of garlic and tomatoes filled the air. I heard the crunch of smashed ice and saw Messi scoop up a couple of handfuls of fish parts from the sink.

Now, the kitchen was beginning to heat up with steam and the smell of fish.

I walked over to the pot and looked in. "What are you making?"

"Fisherman's soup."

"Duh! I thought it was a steak."

"No clams. I promise."

"What are those white things?"

"Bay scallops. You'll love 'em."

"What's the broth made from?"

"Lobster shells and other stuff."

He poured something into a mixing bowl and used a battery-powered hand-blender to mix it. I retreated to the small table. I was now truly in a bind. Messi had gone to so much trouble, I was afraid I'd wind up offending him by turning up my nose. I looked around to see if there would be a way of my dumping his creation without his seeing. No dice. He was such a neat freak there was no place to hide anything.

"I thought you were going to make me pasta," I said plaintively.

"Next time. "

He threw a few small, red-skinned potatoes into the pot, squeezed a lemon, grated something else. I decided not to ask any more questions. I'd do the best I could. Another glass of wine would help. A vodka would even be better.

While the pot boiled, Messi puttered around, scrubbing the cutting board, sharpening the knives, sponging down the entire kitchen area. Even mopping the floor.

Once or twice, I asked if I could help, but he just shook his head, and continued working, seeming as happy as I had ever seen him.

When he'd finished tidying up, he took out a large enamel soup ladle, similar to one my grandmother had, dished his masterpiece into two large bowls and carried them over. He went back into the kitchen for a nice-looking olive bread, two soup spoons and a butter knife, tearing off two pieces of the loaf and handing one to me.

He poured us each a glass of wine, and we clicked glasses. "*C'ent anni.*"

I could feel his eyes on me as I gamely tried a spoonful of his soup.

"Wonderful!" I lied. Truthfully, it wasn't as terrible as I'd feared. I pretended all the white things floating around were potatoes, but the vision of the lobster shells seeped in who-knows-what was a problem.

"I knew you'd like it!" he said.

I did the best I could, which was to eat about half of it. It was no worse than the pink borscht my grandmother used to force on me, but that was bad enough.

At last, Messi looked at his watch, announced it was getting late, and said he had to prepare for his catch the following day. We climbed back into the dingy and paddled back to shore.

I was disappointed that I wouldn't be needing my toothbrush for a sleepover, but he had his priorities, and business before pleasure seemed to be one of them.

I climbed into the car next to him and put on my seat belt.

Now that we had gone through so many intimate experiences together—breaking bread together might even count higher than sex with him—I felt it was time to try to elicit a little more information.

"So, I've eaten your fish soup—and, delicious as it was—I think it merits a little quid pro quo. How about you tell me what's going on between you and Bill Bronson?"

Messi sighed. "You remember I told you we can't fire the sheriff because he knows where the bodies are buried? Well, one of them he buried himself. Me and Hawkeye saw him do it. This goes back. There was a woman walkin' along the road by the shore. I don't know what happened, maybe she moved too far out in the road, maybe the sheriff drinks too much. Whatever.

"Point is, his car hits this lady and, too bad for the sheriff, there's Hawkeye and me, walkin' up the road at that very moment, on our way to get a couple of beers in town. Worse for the sheriff, Hawkeye has his camera, which naturally he puts to use, takin' photos, while I go over and try to help. I can see right away she's deader than a shark's eye, head squashed in like a tomato. Poor woman, I'm okay with dead fish but can't say I have much experience with dead people. Hawkeye stops taking pictures right away.

"The sheriff, well, he starts pleading for me to help him drag her off the road into the bushes. I'm about ready to call 911 and get some backup from the Sands End police, but Bronson, he grabs my arm and says I got to be quiet about this, he'll make it up to me. He's almost blubbering. Says he'll be ruined. Needs a boat to get rid of the body. But no way I'm doing that, putting a bloody body in my boat."

"You said he buried her. Where did he bury her?"

"Can't say for sure. We didn't stick around for that."

"But you didn't turn him in either. A person can't just disappear. Didn't anyone miss her? Post a query in the newspaper?"

Messi shrugged. "Pilgrims Landing, Bliss Bay, Sands End. I know most of the families who live in the East End. But there are lots of strange things that wash up on the shore—flotsam and jetsam. Broken bottles, dead fish, half-eaten bodies the sharks left over. I work nights and I see some parts of life that the so-called good people keep hidden. Where they go for entertainment is none of my business."

"You mean a prostitute?

Messi nodded.

"No matter who she was, she was a person, a human being who deserved something better than dying on a dark lonely road and getting tossed into the sea to be eaten by sharks."

"I don't understand. Why did you just let the sheriff get away with it?"

"She was already dead. I saw an opportunity to get something on him, and I did."

I was trying to get a grip on Messi's peculiar sense of morality, to understand him. "Some people would call that blackmail."

"Call it what you want. It's worked for me. And now hopefully it'll work for you."

There was something missing in this story. I wasn't quite sure what it was. Why was Messi so eager to get something on the sheriff? Why would he need that kind of leverage? An innocent man doesn't try to blackmail a cop.

"What does Bill Bronson have on you?"

Messi snorted, either amused or annoyed by my persistence. "Okay, this all happened two years ago, a few weeks after Marna drowned. The sheriff and me had never gotten along. We were just oil and water. Anyway, he started rumors that I had murdered her. Then he arrested me. Everyone knew she and I had spent time together—that she'd slept at my place on the cliff. Truth is, he might have been able to bring me to trial, if not for the fact they never found a body. So, when I stood next to Bill Bronson by the side of that road that night, you could say an arrangement to help each other avoid the law served us both pretty well."

We spent the rest of the ride in silence. I thought of all my years in New York City and all the people I knew—of all colors and ethnicity—who managed to negotiate their safety from the law. Messi could take his place with any one of them. So, I thought, could Letitia Rose, Hal and a few other fine citizens of the East End. The problem, I realized, was me. I still couldn't let go of my Norman Rockwell picture of America.

I was the true innocent abroad. Or an innocent broad.

We pulled up to the house, and Messi helped me out of the car and walked me to the door.

"You ask too many questions. Everyone in Pilgrim's Landing has a backstory. Some are darker than others. After a while, you'll learn to tell the difference."

And then he kissed me.

For better or worse, learning Messi's backstory didn't seem to make any difference in my desire for his company—or his body. I found myself asking him if he wanted to come in for a while.

He didn't say no.

***

Notes from Sandra Nussbaum, assistant librarian
Fisherman's Stew
Striped bass
Garlic (lots!)
Olive oil
Tomatoes
Wine (some for the chef and some for the pot and some for me)
Broth (ugh!) made from pulverized lobster shells

Taste: Okay accompanied by lots of wine. Would be better with vodka

CHAPTER TWELVE

"How little we know of what there is to know."

—**Ernest Hemingway**, *For Whom the Bell Tolls*

W hat was that? I was suddenly wide awake, sitting straight up in my bed.

There it was again. Someone was turning the knob of my front door, trying to get in!

"Ellen? Ellen? Is that you?"

There was no answer.

The only other person who would visit me in the middle of the night was Messi.

"Messi, is that you?"

A male voice answered: "Yes. Messi. There's been an accident. Let me in!"

Whoever the person outside my door was, it was not Messi. My eyesight might not be great, but my hearing was A-okay. Not only did that voice not belong to Messi, neither did the faint knocking at the door. More like a dog's scratch than Messi's pounding. I was glad my New York habits had stuck, and I had locked the door of the cottage.

Strange what people do in times of high stress. First thing I did was grab my kimono and slip it on, so my dead body would not be discovered naked.

I grabbed my phone and dialed 911, but I knew if whoever it was outside really wanted to get inside, I'd be dead long before the police arrived. A sharp rock to any one of the small windows in the cottage would have broken a pane. By code, the windows had to be big enough for a person to crawl in or out of in case of fire.

Old man Jensen might have been just a fisherman but, like most of the people in Pilgrim's Landing, he obeyed the law. I reached down on the floor for a stiletto-heeled shoe, but only came up with a flip-flop. I had stashed the stilettos in the bathroom since the sheriff's raid. Then my eye roamed over the bookshelf in the bedroom.

The Encyclopedia Britannica! Of course! Every house in America must have owned a set of the Encyclopedia Britannica at one time or another. Big—hard-covered! The perfect weapon in a crisis!

I held the book high in my hand and tried to follow the sounds outside.

I'd left the bedroom window open four or five inches for some fresh air, and now I saw a pair of gloved hands curled beneath the bottom, lifting it up. As soon as the window was fully open, I flung the book with all my strength at the silhouette on the other side! A few papers fell out of the book as it sailed out the window, and there was a thud, followed almost immediately by a grunt. I screamed as loudly as I could: "Help! Murder! Help!"

I doubted anyone would hear—we were deep in the woods—but at least the cottage wasn't padded for sound like the library. Whether any of my neighbors heard me I couldn't say but within minutes there was a very loud siren, flashing lights, the screech of brakes. The sheriff himself had arrived! He and his squashed-nose deputy wasted no time at all bashing in my door and rushing in. They stood there before me, asking if I was okay.

I pulled my kimono more securely around me.

"I'm fine," I said. "Just a little scared, is all."

"Tell us exactly what happened."

"Please. Sit down. Both of you. Let me get you something to drink. A beer maybe?"

"We're on duty, as you can well see, Miss Nussbaum."

At that point, a sweet-faced young man in a police uniform came in with the encyclopedia in his hand. Was he the same kid who had stopped us on the road the other day? It seemed to me, yes.

I held out my hand as he approached with the book.

The sheriff shook his head. "Matthew. Give it here, please. That's evidence. Might have fingerprints—actually, I think there may even be blood on the edge over here. Good aim, Miss Nussbaum."

I have to say I took a cue from my friends Messi and Hawkeye. Before the sheriff could object, I picked up my iPhone and took a quick photo of the Encyclopedia Britannica, volume 1 A, a couple of its torn pages sticking out, and a little red blood on the binding.

Then I quickly picked up the papers that had fluttered to the floor when I flung the book, and I stuffed them into the pocket of my kimono.

When I looked up again, I saw the young guy mumbling something to the sheriff.

"My deputy here, has found the prints of two rather large boots that made quite an impression in the soft mud outside your window. Must be that terrorist A-rab, Issem, lurking about, looking for a victim. It's too bad your friend Messi wasn't around."

And with that, the sheriff and Squashed Nose took their leave. "Better get your door fixed, Miss Nussbaum. You never know who might wander in when no one's around."

I went back into the bedroom, closed the door, and wedged a chair under the knob.

I guess I was having a delayed reaction to the whole episode because I suddenly felt dizzy and my hands began to tremble. I lay down on the bed for a couple of minutes and tried to make sense of my situation.

I'd almost forgotten all about the papers I had stuffed into the pockets of my kimono but when I sat up on the bed, I felt them.

I moved close to the light on my night table and spread them out.

The ink was very faded, and what I thought was paper wasn't paper at all but some kind of parchment or fabric, something I was unfamiliar with. There was a very official-looking seal stamped in gold that had not faded. It seemed to be a deed of some sort made out to Frank Haley Jensen. And the date! Could it be? The date was 1655! Beneath the seal was a map—it looked like an ancient forerunner of the map I'd seen in Job's office. There were squiggly lines and little blocks of color here and there with various names spelled out. All along the sides were trees, and here and there was something that actually looked like a church.

There were two other similar-looking documents. I could read the words "tax" on each, and see that they were made out to the same person, in the years 1656 and 1657!

Grateful that my rough handling of these documents hadn't seemed to harm them, I laid them out on top of my bed to straighten them out. I took Vol. 2 B off the shelf that held the rest of the volumes of the Encyclopedia Britannica. It had a copyright date of 1905. I figured the whole set might be worth a few hundred bucks. I picked up each book in turn and shook it but there were no other documents hidden in the pages.

For the first time, I wondered who actually owned this small cottage. I had rented it from an agent in town. Everyone knew it as The Old Jensen Place. Were there any Jensen descendants still around?

If so, these documents would belong to him. Unlike the encyclopedia, I thought they might fetch real money in the rare book market. The person who would certainly be able to answer some of these questions would be my old friend Winston. I put the documents into Vol. 2 of the Encyclopedia Britannica, and put the book in a large canvas bag, which I deposited by the door. Then I turned off the light next to my bed, and, as the first light began to brighten the sky, I finally fell asleep.

***

I called in sick the next day. I was exhausted and still shaken up by the events of the previous night.

Since I didn't have enough energy to do the laundry or sweep the floor, I figured I'd try to find out who really owned this cottage and maybe do a good deed by giving them the unexpected windfall of what might prove to be valuable documents.

I called up the Chamber of Commerce. They'd been the ones to rent me the cottage. Surely, they'd have some information on the owner's identity.

"The Old Jensen Place? Yes, of course, I know it," Judy, the agent, told me. "Hold on a minute. I'll go look it up."

In a couple of minutes, she had the answer. "The owner of record is Sailor's Cove Realty, registered in Key West."

Key West! That was where Messi spent his winters. If Pilgrim's Landing was the seat of correctness, Key West was the land of "Anything Goes."

"Do you have a name of a person? Who do you send the money to?"

"I just send the rent along to the address I have. I don't have a name."

"Can you give me the address? A phone number?"

"Sure. Thirty-five Dolphin Drive. Hold on. I have a telephone number."

She gave me a phone number with a Florida area code. I was excited. I felt like the announcer for the state lottery, about to award a grand prize to some unsuspecting lucky person. I dialed the number and got an answering machine. A metallic voice said, "We can't answer the phone right now. Please leave a message."

I left my name and cell number and hung up.

Then I went back to sleep.

Sometime in the afternoon, I was awakened by the ringing of my cell phone. I thought it might be the realty company but instead it was Ellen calling from the library to ask how I was feeling.

The sheriff had already visited the library to let everyone know what a great job he was doing protecting all the citizens—especially me.

She seemed more frightened than I was, as I related the details.

"My God, Sandy. It might have been the murderer. Weren't you terrified?"

"I was, but it didn't really hit me till later. When you're actually in a life-or-death situation, you're just trying to survive. Now I'm scared, but I also want answers."

The sheriff didn't know about the documents I'd found tucked into the encyclopedia, but I found myself telling Ellen about them.

"I found a deed, too!" she said. "In a cookie jar! My dad did some farming for some of the old families, odd jobs during the winter. But he won a plot of land in a poker game. Took me to see it once. A big field in the middle of Bliss Bay, not far from the town dump. Wasn't worth much in those days. But he always said we should never sell it. It was only for an emergency—a rainy day.

"And then he died in 1957, and he had only told my mom where he hid the deed, and then my mom got Alzheimer's and I never did find it. I figured Dad must have paid taxes on the property, that the town would have a record. But this all happened before computers, and nobody seemed to have anything with our name on it, save the house we live in. But last night, in the bottom of our old cookie jar, I found the deed! It was dated 1955 and there was a map showing five acres, between Elm Street and Walnut Street. Except that it's no longer an empty lot. That 5-acre lot between Elm Street and Walnut Street is right in the middle of the Bliss Bay Shopping Center!"

"But your dad must have sold it at some point. The deed you found can't still be valid."

"I don't know. My dad wasn't one of those three-namers you talk about, but he grew up in a Pilgrim town with all the Pilgrim values. Trust me on this one. Taking care of family and saving money for a rainy day was as much a part of the town culture as going to church on Sunday. He never sold that lot!"

If what she was saying was true, my friend Ellen was going to be a very rich woman! Unless the town had foreclosed on the lot because, after her dad died, no one paid the taxes.

"Didn't you ever get some notice from the town about taxes due?"

"No. I had kind of given up trying to claim the property until I found the deed in the cookie jar."

"It seems to me we need to go to town hall and check these documents against what they have on file."

Even as I said it, I knew this would not be as easy as it seemed. I knew that the sheriff, Job, and Winston were all town trustees, and none of them could be fully trusted to tell the truth.

"Job is in charge of records. I think Job will tell us the truth. We were once... friends."

I wouldn't give a fig for that friendship today, I thought, though I didn't say it. "Let me bring Messi when we go," I said. "He isn't directly involved in any of this. And the sheriff is afraid of him. He could come in handy."

Ellen said she would meet us at town hall.

I looked at my watch. Messi should be getting up about this time. I called him on his cell:

"Sandy, my sweet, I was just about to head out on the boat."

"I need your help."

"Unless this is an emergency—"

"I believe it is. "

There was some mumbling on his end and then he said, "I'll be at your cottage in ten minutes."

Then I called Job.

"So glad I caught you. Ellen and I need to look up something at the records office. I know the record office closes at five, but this is kind of an emergency. And I think you're gonna want to see the documents I've found before I show them to the sheriff."

That seemed to convince Job. He told us to meet him there in thirty minutes.

Then I called the sheriff.

"Ellen and I have some new evidence on that murderer you're looking for. Did you get a match yet for the blood on the book?"

He said he hadn't.

"Well, maybe we can help. Meet us at town hall in half an hour. Job is going to show us some old records."

I waited in front of the house for Messi. Then I climbed into the car beside him and filled him in on the plan as we drove into town.

CHAPTER THIRTEEN

"We need the tonic of wildness.... At the same time that we are
earnest to explore and learn all things, we require that all things
be mysterious and unexplorable, that land and sea be indefinitely
wild, unsurveyed and unfathomed by us because unfathomable.
We can never have enough of nature."

—Henry David Thoreau, *Walden*

"So, what exactly are you looking for?" Job sat behind one of the desks
in the town hall records room. It was here that beach permits, parking
permits and building permits were issued; here, too, that deeds of sale were
recorded, and taxes were paid.

Job Abraham Farrington was a trustee of the town almost by reason of his
birth, but as a war hero he had been legitimately elected to his post as chief officer
of the records department. He rolled out from behind the desk now, looking
every inch the hero, in his navy whites and gold-brocaded officer's cap, with his
purple heart medal from Afghanistan pinned to the breast of the jacket.

I had never seen Job dressed in his navy whites before. He'd told me he hated
war and everything related to it, as well he should. It had ruined his life.

Perhaps he thought we'd come for a "shaming" session, and this was his armor to ward it off. Whatever he might have thought, he met my gaze directly and greeted Ellen with a friendly nod.

He seemed surprised to see Messi there but shook his hand and met his eyes, too, like the true soldier that he was.

When the sheriff arrived with his squashed-nose deputy, the atmosphere changed, particularly when he laid eyes on Messi.

"What's he doing here?" the sheriff complained. "He doesn't even live in Pilgrim's Landing! And what's this all about?"

Ellen handed Job the document she'd found.

"I've finally located the deed to a plot of land my dad won years ago in a poker game. It's for five acres in Bliss Bay, between Elm Street and Walnut Street, dated 1955. I know my dad never sold that empty lot and yet, somehow, that piece of property is now a major part of the Bliss Bay Shopping Mall. We're here to see how that could have happened."

Job picked up the deed and rolled back behind his desk. He took a key out of the top drawer and rolled over to a large filing cabinet in one corner of the room. He flipped through a number of papers until he found the one he wanted. He pulled it out and gave it to Ellen.

"According to our records, this piece of property was sold in 1957."

"Who bought it?" Ellen asked.

"It says right here." He pointed to a name on the document. "The Conscience Crossing Realty Company."

Ellen looked at the deed, then handed it back to Job. She shook her head. "I know my father never sold that property. "

Messi took the deed out of her hand and asked, "Who's the CEO of that company?"

Job shrugged. "Hard to say. It would take some time to track down who that person is."

Messi shook his head. "Now Joby, my friend, you and I have recorded many pieces of property all over the East End of Long Island. You have a record of the owner right there in your drawer. You need to have a person's name on record for tax bills. So why don't you save yourself embarrassment and tell us the name of the CEO of Conscience Crossing Realty."

The sheriff stepped forward. "You stay out of this. You shouldn't even be in this room. Jail's a more suitable place for you. Protecting terrorists!"

But Job was in charge here and he rolled back to his desk. Then he turned around and faced us.

"The CEO of that company is Job Abraham Farrington."

"Thank you," Messi said.

Ellen walked over to the desk and stared at Job. "So how do you explain the fact that my father never sold it to you?"

Job grasped the side of the desk and attempted to stand. But he gave up and sank back down into his wheelchair.

"I explain it like this. I was born in this town. My father and his father and his father were born in this town. We were all born in this town going back hundreds of years. I grew up with a girl I loved. Her name was Ellen Hinkley. When her father died, I paid the taxes on that property. I was going to give it to Ellen as a wedding gift. I believed she loved me, too. And then I went to war. Answered the call of my country like the stupid, ignorant boy that I was. And when I came back, a cripple and good for nothing, this girl, Ellen Hinkley, did not want me. And to tell you the truth, who could blame her? Nobody wants a cripple! And so, I thought, this town, this country, this girl owes me something. I saw an opportunity for revenge. And I took it. I knew her father had hidden that deed. I knew he'd told her never to sell it. She'd spoken to me about it many times. So, I knew she wouldn't know that it had been taken—stolen—from her, from someone she once called her friend."

And then, while we all watched spellbound, Job reached into the desk drawer, took out a gun and put it to his head.

Messi was closest. He lunged toward Job, knocking the gun out of his hand and sending it skittering across the floor

. The two of them landed on the floor, with Job's wheelchair knocked over on its side. My heart was beating so fast I thought I would pass out. Ellen began to cry.

The sheriff grabbed the gun from the floor, then moved toward them, handcuffs at the ready.

Messi got to his feet, holding up his hand.

"Not yet, Sheriff. Ellen's found a few more documents that need clarification."

Ellen took a deep breath, gathering herself, then handed the maps she'd found in Eddie's strongbox to the sheriff. "If you look closely, you can see how each one of these maps is almost the same, but not quite. In each of them, a portion of property is being transferred from the Montgomery property to Conscience Crossing Realty."

Messi looked over at the sheriff and then back at Job. "Joby, my friend. You are the CEO of Conscience Crossing, but not the only officer. There is also a CFO, and do you see that person in the room?"

Before Job could utter a word, the sheriff took out his own gun and pointed it straight at Job's heart.

How could this be happening in Pilgrim's Landing? I'd spent my whole life in New York City and had only experienced one small mugging. I'd never even seen a gun until I came here! But this was happening so quickly, I didn't know who to look at or where to take cover if the shooting started. My main thought was to fly out the door, but just as I thought that, I heard the click of a revolver and turned to see Squashed Nose aim his gun smack at the middle of the Sheriff's back.

"Thank you, Eugenio. I knew I could count on you," Messi said. "Bill Bronson, I'd drop that gun if I were you. We have a tape of this entire proceeding. You see, Eugenio here is actually a federal agent."

Holy shit! There was so much going on, for a moment, I forgot to be scared. Messi was so cool! I felt as if I were watching an old western.

Job said, "The sheriff is the CFO of Conscience Crossing Realty."

Instead of dropping his gun, the sheriff pivoted around, and I found myself staring down the black hole of the barrel.

Instinct took over. I hit the floor and rolled into a ball.

Everyone started moving at once.

There was a clatter of chairs skidding across linoleum and the roar of a gunshot. I'd never actually heard a gunshot in real life, only in the movies, and if I hadn't already been rolled up into a ball and hugging the floor, the noise alone would have knocked me over.

When I summoned the courage to open my eyes, I was greeted by the sight of Messi punching the sheriff and knocking him to the ground.

Job's gun, the one the sheriff had snagged from the floor, landed close to my head. I was terrified by the sight of it, but somehow I summoned the willpower to pick it up.

I had never touched a gun before, and I held it as far away from my body as possible, surprised by the weight of it, hoping it wouldn't suddenly go off. Messi held down the sheriff, who was cursing up a storm that grew even louder after the squashed nosed deputy managed to handcuff his hands behind his back.

Ellen had landed on the floor right next to me, and we both got up and brushed ourselves off. Happily, I did not see any blood anywhere except on the sheriff's face near where Messi had punched him.

With the sheriff handcuffed, Messi stood up, and went over to the fallen Job, putting his hand out to help him back into his wheelchair. "Sorry to do this, old friend, but I got a few deeds of my own to add on."

I knew that Job was a pretty cool customer under fire. I knew he wouldn't have rolled himself into a ball like yours truly. Even if he was a crook, I still had a grudging admiration for him—he was a war hero, after all.

Life had dealt him a lousy hand, and I was glad that Messi, at least, showed him some fragments of respect.

Messi pulled a bunch of papers from his backpack. "You see, you were playing around with Shinnecock lands, too. That's a federal offense. A few of you are going to jail. And a couple, namely the ones who murdered Eddie and Pepe, are likely to be there for a long, long time."

Job shook his head. "I never murdered anyone, Messi. I swear it!"

Could any of us believe anything Job or the Sheriff said? I really can't say. I certainly couldn't think straight in the moment. All I really wanted was to get the hell out of there as quickly as possible.

Messi said to Job: "Now that you've come clean and—what do they call it—turned state's evidence—maybe my friend Eugenio here can give you some kind of a break in this Indian business, at least. We don't have another pair of handcuffs, so I do hope you'll get into the car on your own and let the deputy lock you up in town. Ellen came in her own car, and I know she can drive herself home. I've got to take this confused librarian back to the old Jensen place."

Confused was probably an understatement at this point. I began to tremble again, as it sunk in that I had nearly witnessed a suicide and a murder, with me as at least one of the murder victims.

Why did these things happen to me? I'd come to Pilgrim's Landing seeking peace and regeneration, but that ship had apparently sailed. Maybe it was me. Maybe I brought bad karma with me wherever I went. All I knew was that I was so traumatized by everything that had happened that Messi had to half-carry me into his small car and drive me back to the cottage on Frogs Neck Road.

Once we were there, he set me down in the bedroom. With my head on the pillow, I heard him out in the kitchen, dropping ice cubes into a glass. He came back holding a glass of vodka in each hand—he'd remembered! After putting the drinks down on the small night table next to my bed, he bounced up and down on the edge of the mattress.

"You can really use a better mattress. This one is sure to give you a backache. Much too soft."

He got up and roamed around the room, stopping to open and close the window the prowler had lifted to try to get in. Finally, he came to rest at the sagging bookshelves holding the set of the Encyclopedia Britannica.

He took one of the books off the shelf. "I bet you had a set like this in Brooklyn when you were growing up."

"Of course. We had everything in Brooklyn. I remember cutting up one of the volumes to make a book report. My mother had a fit."

"Well. I did not have an encyclopedia Britannica. We tended more towards Sears Roebuck catalogues. It's a wonder I learned anything at all."

I took a long swallow of my vodka. It felt warm and smooth going down my throat. I stopped trembling. Messi left his glass on the table and took out a joint. He took a couple of puffs and then lay down next to me.

"Where do you get that stuff? It's still against the law."

"Yes and no. I have a special dispensation. Medical marijuana. Me and my friend Job. I got a couple of metal rods and screws stuck there in my left leg. Pains me mostly when I stand watch on the boat too long. That's one of the things that brought us together. "

I pictured all those ashtrays in Messi's boat, and I wondered what else Messi was bringing in besides medical marijuana. Cuban cigars, for sure.

I finished my drink and lay down on the bed. "Do you think Job murdered Eddie and Pepe because they found out that he was forging all those documents?"

"I don't think so. A forger and a crook, okay. I know he killed his share in the war. But taking out a neighbor? I don't think so. It's more likely the sheriff did it or hired someone. It feels good to finally be able to get rid of him."

"Where did this Eugenio character come from? Is he really a mute? How long have you been planning this, this... sting operation?"

"Remember, I told the sheriff that all kinds of people work on a fishing boat? Eugenio needed a job, and I needed a strong guy, so I gave him what he needed, and he gave me what I needed—loyalty. Best as I can figure out, he was deserted by his mom and left by the side of the road. Never could talk but wasn't stupid at all. Spent some time in a boxing ring at Sands End. He was good, too. But no real future in it—and he took a lot of punishment. So, after he worked for me, I helped get him a job as an undercover guy with the Feds. Perfect cover. No one would peg him for anything other than Mr. Smashed Nose."

"Amazing! I just don't understand how you manage these things!"

Messi put his joint down on the night table and turned off the light. "How do you manage to remember all the names of all those characters in all those books you read? It comes with the territory."

***

When I woke up the next morning, Messi was gone. No surprise there. As he had told me on several occasions, he had to make a living. Whatever else he might be, Neptune, Satan, pirate or Tarzan of the sea, he was first and foremost, a fisherman.

I got up and made myself a pot of coffee, contemplating the bashed-in-door to my cottage while I sat there in my little kitchen. Fixing the door would be expensive now that Ellen was no longer engaged to the founder of the biggest hardware business in the East End, and I couldn't get a discount.

Even though I was alone, I was feeling pretty safe with both Job and the sheriff behind bars, and I couldn't help wonder what else, besides the deed, I might find in my small cottage. So, I decided to take a look around before I dressed for work.

Long Island is really flat and subject to floods and surges of the tides when conditions are ripe, so many of the houses along the shore have no real basements—just crawl spaces. I had no real idea what was under this cottage, but I was curious, given recent developments, and I was feeling lucky.

Maybe old Mr. Jensen had some other treasures I might uncover.

I pulled on a pair of jeans and a t-shirt and walked outside, looking for some doorway or entrance. I figured there must be a place for a hot water heater, a furnace, and whatever else was involved in heating up a year-round domicile.

Because there was so much water, not only in the bay and ocean but just in the air, most of the houses in the area didn't have conventional basements.

They would keep an oil tank and winter clothes in a nearby garage or shed. I walked around the house a couple of times until I saw a wooden basement door half hidden by tall grass. I was able to lift it enough for a small furry rat to scurry out—but no further because it was padlocked.

I went back inside and started to get dressed for the library.

Hello. What's this?

As I reached into the closet for my trousers, I noticed a raised area on the floor of the closet. I picked up my iPhone with its flashlight and after just a gentle jiggle or two, a couple of the floorboards came loose. Beneath was a small space which held a metal strongbox. I carried the box to the bed. It opened easily. Inside was a closely packed package of what looked to me like marijuana tobacco.

It must have weighed a couple of pounds. What was it worth? I had no idea. I was pretty sure, though, that Messi would know.

I replaced the package in the metal box and closed the lid, then placed the box back in the trap and covered it with the two boards.

Now, more than ever, I wanted to know who owned this cottage. Maybe the prowler wasn't Eddie's and Pepe's killer at all, but someone who needed to scare off whoever had rented the place so he could access his stash.

The quickest answer to these questions was to ask Winston. He was the head of the library's research department, and he had lived long enough in this town to know the intimate history of most everyone in it.

I knew he was involved in some way in the forgery scheme, but he wasn't one of the officers of that Conscience Crossing Corporation, and it was hard for me to believe that he could have had much of a role in anything. He'd always been so friendly towards me.

I slipped into my black slacks and white no-iron shirt, combed my hair, and got ready to go to the library. Ellen and I were usually the first to arrive, so we could open up. Letitia Rose didn't come in until 10:00. Winston? He hadn't answered his phone all day yesterday. That usually meant he was hung over, big time. He might be home—another crumbling mansion high on the hill overlooking the ocean—or he might have slept at the library, which he often did.

I closed the bashed-in-door of my cottage as best I could (I had nothing of value inside except the pearl Messi had given me, which I now carried in the pocket of my trousers) and drove to the library, parking in the lot on the side.

I was pleased to see Winston's car in its place, under the old oak tree. I unlocked the library doors and walked downstairs to the lower level.

Sure enough, there was Winston, slumped over in his desk chair, his long white hair covering his face. His office was more unkempt than usual. There was a half-eaten hot dog on the floor near his desk, a squashed coffee cup that hadn't quite made it into the wastepaper basket, and, on the stool next to him, his silver flask. His muddy boots lay on their side near the door. His face was unshaven and looked red and slightly swollen.

I was about to leave—there didn't seem to be much point in trying to have an intelligent conversation with someone so obviously hung over—when Winston suddenly groaned, opened his eyes, and lifted his head.

"My dear Sandra. I'm so sorry. I must have fallen asleep—up late last night...."

His voice trailed off, and he ran his hand through his hair in an attempt to make it presentable. He pushed it this way and that, but it ended up all bunched to one side, like a wig that had slipped from its proper place. And then he spied his boots across the room.

Clearly embarrassed, partly because one of his socks had a hole in it, he made a valiant effort to rise from his desk and totter over to the door. He motioned for me to follow, and holding on to my shoulder, he slipped on one boot and then the other.

"Now, my dear young lady. So sorry you had to see me in this state of undress, but I hope you will forgive an old man. What can I do for you?"

I pulled the documents out of my bag. "You know I'm renting the old Jensen cottage?"

"On Frogs Neck Road."

I didn't think it was necessary to worry him with an account of my midnight visitor—who probably was now behind bars anyway—and so I skipped to the chase. "I noticed there was a complete set of the Encyclopedia Britannica on the shelf in the bedroom, so I picked up one of the volumes to check the copyright date and guess what I found? It was published in 1905!"

Winston beamed. "How exciting! And you say there was a complete set? If the condition is good that could bring in several hundred dollars. hat Lucky you! The library has a set from 1910, I believe—up there on the top shelf."

"There's more. When I opened the cover of the book, guess what I found right inside?"

I handed him the three documents I had brought.

Winston took them and moved back to his desk. He picked up a magnifier and turned on one of his special lamps.

"1655! What an amazing find! These papers are worth a small fortune. I bet the library would buy them. I can speak to the Montifiore brothers. They own the tennis club in Pilgrim's Landing and they're on the board!"

He opened the top drawer of his desk, but I reached out my hand before he could tuck them away.

"I appreciate your help in all this Winston, but I don't own these documents. They belong to the Jensen family."

Winston lifted the documents out of my reach. He got up and locked the door to his office.

"Listen to me, Sandra. The Jensen family is long gone. The last Jensen never married and had no heirs. The town auctioned the property. As far as I am concerned—and I am a trustee of this town—you own these papers."

"But what about the person who bought the property? Doesn't he own all the furniture and everything else in it?"

I took hold of one end of the documents while Winston kept hold of the other. I began to wonder if I would have to wrestle him for them.

"Whoever bought the cottage isn't local. I think it was some company based in Key West. Listen to me. No one will be the wiser. These papers belong in Pilgrim's Landing."

I must admit, this all seemed very tempting. Winston believed there was one code of behavior for people in Pilgrim's Landing, and another for everyone outside. But there was something fishy about this transaction. And the Key West connection set off a set of warning bells in my head.

"Does anyone else know about this discovery?"

I nodded. "Ellen...Messi..."

Winston smiled and put his arm around me. "Ellen, I held her on my lap when she was a baby. She'll be okay. Now Messi. Messi could be a problem. I know he's a friend of yours, but he's not a man of good character. He killed that Marna Van Dugan. I know he did. She was pregnant with the child of Letty's son, Luke. Luke died of an overdose. He had to kill her. The scandal would have ruined too many people."

Letitia Rose had a son! I remembered now when she had emptied her purse. There was a photo of a handsome light-skinned boy! So that was the connection between Letitia Rose and Messi. That was one piece of his back-story that he had neglected to tell me.

But I was here on other business, and my eyes were slowly beginning to open.

"Don't worry about Messi. I can take care of him when the time comes. Listen to me. I admire your rectitude, your desire to do the right thing. Of course. We all want to do that. It's really easy. We can sell these documents and replace them with copies!"

"Copies? You can make good copies of these documents?"

"Yes! Yes! My dear, can you keep a secret? I know you're a good girl. Job and me, we have been copying old documents for years!"

"And nobody's found out?"

"Of course not. No one will find out. We sell the real documents to the rare book dealers who might be able to tell a copy from the real thing. We put the copies back where we found them—in these cartons still wrapped up from the old library."

Winston waved his hand at a couple of boxes in the far corner of his office. One of them was open. One of them was taped closed and secured with a thick rope.

Winston walked over to the sealed box, whipped out a pocket-knife from his side pocket, and in an instant cut through the heavy rope.

Oh my God! What was I thinking? Actually, what had I *not* been thinking! When Winston bent over to open that box, the hair that had been hiding one side of his face moved away and I saw a scab and a red-blue bruise on his forehead!

Of course! The muddy boots! The bruise! Worst of all—the knife that I now saw clearly was the murder weapon! It was Winston who was the prowler I'd hit with the book! It was Winston who had come upstairs after Pepe was murdered. He claimed he had heard us all stomping about, but the library was padded for noise control.

And there—in the corner of his office, under a couple of empty coffee cups, was a bonnet, and a black skirt! The very outfit of the phony ghost!

Winston cut quickly through the tape and lifted up a handful of papers.

"Look, my dear! All these documents! Stuffed for five years in these cartons, getting moldy. I have saved them for posterity! Job and I have studied them and made beautiful copies. Nicer even then the originals. And no one will know. Even when someone finally unpacks all these cartons. Only these two have valuable papers. No one really cares. No one has my knowledge! They will be stored in files for scholars' years from now to peruse. And they will take down the information but will never check the authenticity. The documents kept at the Pilgrim's Landing library are internationally known to be authentic!"

Whether Winston read the horrified expression on my face, or he suddenly realized that now that he had confessed his crime, he would have to kill me, I will never know. What I do know is he suddenly put down the papers he had been holding and pointed his knife in my direction.

I backed away from him and moved quickly towards his big desk. In a couple of steps, Winston had caught up with me. I felt my back now against the large wall of books on his sagging shelves.

"Winston. I understand perfectly. We can be partners. We can work together. I can take care of Messi! I'll tell him you said the papers I found were fake."

"I'm so sorry, Sandra. I really liked you. But I am done with partners. In the end, they want too much. Like Eddie. He wanted more money because he had finally, after all these years, gotten up enough courage to marry Ellen. But he wanted too much. And so I had to get rid of him, and then I had to get rid of poor Pepe because he had seen it all and you... you were the only one new enough to the library to see with clear eyes what was going on... so you, my dear, you...."

I'd backed up so far against the wall of books they were cutting into my t-shirt.

"Letitia Rose! Letitia Rose! We are in here," I yelled.

Winston, momentarily confused, looked at the door instead of me and at that moment, I reached up as high as I could and pulled as hard as I could and the whole bookshelf trembled for an instant and then an avalanche of thick volumes fell down on top of Winston's head and I watched as each volume of, yup—the Encyclopedia Britannica—cascaded down on Winston's skull.

I ducked and crawled away just as the next row came down on top of the first and then the next and then the next and I finally reached the door of Winston's office, unlocked it and moved into the hallway, just in time to collide with Letitia Rose Jefferson!

She was already calling 911 on her iPhone, and we both backed up into the hallway and when I turned around, there was Ellen standing right in back of her, and I fell into their arms.

CHAPTER FOURTEEN

"This was a big storm and he might as well enjoy it."

—**Ernest Hemingway**, *For Whom the Bell Tolls*

"Looks like Winston had an accident," Hal said, as Hawkeye snapped a bunch of photos.

An ambulance had arrived, and two men in white coats came out carrying a stretcher.

"Just a couple more shots, if you please," Hal requested.

Mathew, the deputy in charge, nodded.

There had been no movement under the pile of books, and nobody was in a hurry to save Winston, just in case the books had not done him in. But there was an arm sticking out and the young policeman took his pulse, shook his head and retreated to the hallway.

Letitia Rose smiled. "Now Hawkeye, I do believe you can take another prize-winning photo and we will put it right upstairs on the wall!"

"Be sure and get some close-ups of those books," Letitia Rose directed. "There's *Moby Dick*, right on top, and Hawthorne's *Scarlet Letter*, and on the left is *Huckleberry Finn*."

She moved quickly around the pile, picked up Hemingway's *The Old Man and the Sea* from the floor and placing it front and center on top of the pile.

"That's our Book Club pick this week."

I peeked in from the doorway, not feeling like entering that room ever again. Ellen was right next to me, and I guess she felt the same. This time she actually put her arms around me and gave me a hug.

"I think a good caption for your article could be 'The Revenge of the Books,'" I suggested.

Hal shook his head. "The way I see it, this scion of Pilgrim's Landing has given service to this community for many years. To die, with his boots on—so to speak—at his desk, using his last breath researching the history of the home he loved, yada, yada, yada...."

Talk about fake news! This was a whitewashing of the situation beyond all bearing! This scion of Pilgrim's Landing society had murdered two other people and almost murdered me!

"Now, wait just a minute! You can't possibly make up a lie like that!"

Letitia Rose squeezed my shoulder. "Take a listen, girl. I know you have suffered a terrible trauma in that room. But so has the entire community. Ellen here—she lost her greatest love. The library lost its entire research department and its children's art instructor. What Hal is saying is not a lie. He is telling a partial truth. Think about it for a second. What possible good would it do to throw dirt on the family of one of the founders of our town? "

Hal motioned for us to get closer together, so Hawkeye could get a photo of "The heroines who made the sad discovery."

"Doesn't the truth matter?" I asked Letitia Rose. "He confessed everything to me. He was selling irreplaceable old documents belonging to this library, to this community. He murdered Eddie and Pepe because they knew too much—and he was about to murder me!"

Letitia Rose scowled. "Those moldy old documents? They've been stuffed into cartons for five years and isn't anyone who missed them. In the end, it's people who count. Now Ellen here—it was partly Winston's research work that made that old deed she found so valuable. And Winston? He can't murder anyone else. You have brought down God's judgement upon him.

"Of course, truth matters. But all those dead ancestors—Admiral Winston Halsey Smith—he died in World War I. His uncle lost a leg in World War II. His great, great grandfather fought on the Rebel side during the Civil War. They can't defend their honor, but we can. Winston was the last in his line. He was penniless. He had sold off all the family heirlooms. Let him rest in peace."

I could see her point, although it was hard for me to share it. Few people in New York City had honorable ancestors to protect. And if they were disgraced, they would just move elsewhere.

But in Pilgrim's Landing, you were stuck with what you and your family had done. There didn't seem to be any honorable way out.

"How did you all find me, anyway? The library is padded for sound."

Letitia Rose laughed. "Honey—it might be padded for sound, but when you brought down that shelf of books, it sounded like a volcanic eruption! That set of Encyclopedia Britannica sure did its work! Proves books and outdated types like me can still be useful—even in the age of the internet!"

We left the men in the white coats to uncover Winston. The rest of us started up the stairs to the main reading room.

I held on to Letitia Rose as we climbed. "Winston told me about your son and Marna Van Dugan. I'm so sorry!"

I felt Letitia Rose stiffen. She unhooked my arm from hers. She planted herself in the middle of the staircase so no one could move past us. She pulled herself up to her full height and turned to me.

"My son had nothing whatsoever to do with Marna Van Dugan. And don't you ever forget it!"

We went the rest of the way up in silence.

***

"Now didn't I tell you when we first met to watch your pretty ass in these shark-infested waters? And here I see you all black and blue back there on that beautiful behind."

"I think it was *Moby Dick* whacked my backside!"

We were lying together, naked, in his house on the cliff. The sun was just coming up—or rather—the sun was trying to shine through a bunch of really dark clouds.

"The thing I don't understand is why you went running off to see Winston after Job and the sheriff had practically confessed to murder."

"I still wanted to find out who owned the old Jensen house, and whether or not those documents were real. And then I found a stash of marijuana under a couple of boards in the closet, so I just wanted information that I thought only Winston would have. The truth is, I thought he was too ineffectual to do anything really bad."

Messi got up and started getting dressed. He glanced out the window. "Looks like a storm coming up."

"So why don't you stay home today—with me? I'm sure we can find something to do indoors."

He walked back to the bed and kissed me. "Do you still have those documents? What did Winston say?"

I got up and pulled them out of my canvas overnight bag. Messi took a quick look at them and handed them back to me.

"Winston said they were the real thing. So real he wanted to sell them right away. That's when he decided he had to murder me. Maybe I should have played along. Could have been a rich woman. But they belong to whoever owns the Jensen house, and I still don't know who that is—some corporation in Key West."

Messi smiled and sat down on the bed. He pulled me down next to him.

"That's an easy one. The owner is one Giancarlo Messini."

What can I say? That another small piece of Messi's backstory that he had somehow forgotten to tell me had almost cost me my life?

"Well, one thing I can tell you. I'm not sure what merchandise you might have stored in your basement, but I know some rats live there."

Messi shook his head. "There are no rats in Pilgrim's Landing."

Even though he didn't live here, he'd obviously drunk the Kool-Aid. I was going to leave that one alone.

"So, all for these months I've been paying my rent to you?"

"Yes and no. You were paying it to a corporation in Key West, as you said. I don't keep that money. It goes to a personal charity of mine."

Now I was really getting angry. Who the hell did he think he was? I was sick and tired of this "partial truth" bullshit!

"What kind of 'charity' are you talking about? Are you keeping a wife down there? A girlfriend? Winston said something else, too. He said you had murdered Marla Van Dugan. He knew it. She had been impregnated by Letitia Rose's son Luke, and you had to kill her because you couldn't face the humiliation!"

If I thought a black cloud had covered the sun outside, inside it felt as if a hurricane was about to hit. Messi paused, half-dressed, his turquoise eyes glittering in the dim light. I could see the ripples of his muscles, the scars of his shark bites. He took a deep breath.

"And why would you believe a drunk and a self-confessed murderer?"

"Because Winston never lied to me. He might have been a murderer and a forger, but he was not a liar!"

"When have I lied to you?"

"You don't lie, but you tell half-truths. All of you here in Pilgrim's Landing. You told me everyone has a backstory, and you still haven't told me all of yours!"

"What do you want to know?"

"I want to know what the hell is going on in Key West. It seems to be an inside-out version of Pilgrim's Landing, a hell to its heaven. If Pilgrim's Landing is ruled by long traditions of 'correct behavior' Key West is just the opposite—a place where there are no traditions, no laws, no 'correctness'—a place where anything goes. "

Messi exhaled and continued to dress. He put on a wetsuit, and then a sweatshirt.

"You're right to some degree. People in Key West don't care much for rules and laws. A person can live out his life without all his neighbors passing judgment. Sounds a lot like New York the way you've described the city to me. I don't know why you're so shocked and appalled."

I had to agree that, in some sense, this was true, but I still didn't have his whole backstory and I wanted it.

"And I want to know who owns that stash of marijuana I found under the boards of the closet in that cottage!"

"I do. I told you I can legally use medical marijuana."

I had lost interest in Messi's smuggling activities, if that was something he was into. I was after bigger game.

"I want to know if you killed Marna Van Dugan."

Messi grabbed me then and swung me around to face him. His fingers dug into my arm.

"After all we've been through together! After I saved your life out there in the water! After all our time together, you still don't trust me? You take the word of that piece of shit Winston over me?"

He threw me down on the bed. "Did I ever ask you what men you were with before you met me? Did I ever ask you about the years you spent in your ex-husband's bed? Why can't you accept me as I am?"

For the first time in our relationship, I was afraid of him. I never really believed he had killed her. Maybe, like in *An American Tragedy*, he had somehow, either deliberately or unintentionally, allowed her to drown, but I never really thought he was capable of murder—until that moment. Still, I couldn't leave it alone.

I got up from the bed and stood in front of the door of the bedroom.

"Why won't you answer my question! Did you kill Marna Van Dugan?"

Messi just stared at me. I met his stare and did not look away.

"Do you know why you will not eat a raw clam? Because you don't want to. And because you don't think I have any right to ask you to do what you don't want to do. "

"Don't you think I have a right to an answer? Don't I mean anything to you?"

"You mean a great deal, but you're not everything."

He turned away from me. His shoulders slumped, and I could see the air leak out of him. But then he drew himself up and went over to the corner of the room where he had his emergency travel bag stashed. He opened it and began darting around the room, opening and closing drawers, throwing in this article and that, as if I weren't there. He went into the bathroom and brought out a razor and a bar of soap.

"It's no use. No matter what I do on the East End of Long Island, half the population will believe I murdered Marna Van Dugan, and the other half will be unsure. I thought you would be different."

A sudden clap of thunder shook the house, and a bolt of lightning lit up the sky.

Messi glanced out the window and closed his bag. He hoisted it and carried it into the kitchen.

There was another clap of thunder very close by.

And just as Messi opened the kitchen door, a bolt of lightning struck a large oak tree near the house. The tree swayed and shook, and then, with an eerie wail, a huge branch broke off and fell at Messi's feet.

I followed him, pulling on his shirt. "Don't go out there! Please! Please! I didn't mean it. None of it. I trust you. I love you... please... you'll die in that storm!"

Messi stopped for a moment, his body backlit—truly Neptune himself—the lord of the sea.

"I told you there were no old men or ancient mariners on the sea." And with that, he pulled away from me and loped down the hill towards the dingy.

The heavens opened up then, and the rain came down so heavily I could hardly see, and I slipped and my naked body slid down the path in the mud until I reached the shore. By then, Messi was already gone. So, I just sat there, covered in mud, and cried, my tears blending with the rain. I don't know how long I was there, but the next thing I knew, someone flung a blanket around me, and I saw that it was Hawkeye. He pulled me up, and then half-carried me up the muddy path—our bare-feet squishing the mud as we went, and in the shelter of the kitchen, he sat me down in a chair.

The rain pelted the glass, turning it into a blur, and we waited there silently for the storm to pass. At last, the rain and howling wind and the rumbling died down.

I pulled out my own overnight bag then and slipped into my dark trousers and no-iron white shirt. I pulled out the documents Messi had returned and carefully replaced them in my bag. And then Hawkeye took me out into what was now a light rain and drove me home.

*****

In the early fall, mornings at sunrise, I'd head down to the edge of the shore beneath Messi's cottage on the cliff to look out to sea before I set off for the library. Sometimes Ellen would come with me, and we'd talk of what might have been.

I thought about Messi all the time and wondered if he'd survived that storm. Was he living it up in Key West? I called the number for Sailor's Cove Realty often. It was always the recorded message. And no one ever called me back.

Had he ever loved me? Or had I just been another port in the storm?

I sometimes thought of the last scene in the opera *Peter Grimes*, where Grimes, suspected of terrible crimes, was told to row himself out to sea and not return. Was that what had happened to Messi?

Ellen was a wealthy woman now. An owner of the largest shopping mall on the East End of Long Island. I asked her if she would ever forgive Job. If she would ever maybe even marry him.

She was resolute, shaking her head as looked out to sea.

I wondered who the beneficiary was of that so-called charity Messi set up.

I thought about the documents I found in the old Jensen cottage. Had Messi simply forgotten about them in his rage? Or had he wanted me to have them? A gift to remember him by.

I wondered, too, about the dolphin with the white flipper. Did someone else feed him now? Or did he cruise the sea, searching for Messi?

And so each morning I gazed out at the sea, like all those sea captains' wives before me who had paced widow's walks waiting for their men to return, and I wondered if Messi would be one who did or didn't. And if any of my questions would ever be answered.

EPILOGUE

"Oh, for shame, how the Mortals put the blame on us Gods for they say evil comes from us, but it is they, rather who by their own recklessness win sorrow beyond what is given."

—**Homer**, *The Odyssey*

Thunder. Lightning. Pounding on my door.

I sit straight up in bed. Am I dreaming?

Pitch dark. And then a flash of lightning illuminates the sky.

The electric clock next to my bed is dark. The wires are down.

Pounding on my door. Shouts above a clap of thunder that seems to shake the whole cottage.

"Sandy! For God's Sake! Let me in before I get washed away in the storm!"

Can it be?

I get out of bed, activate the flashlight on my phone, make my way to the closed door.

"Who is it?"

"For God's sake, Sandy! Who do you think it is? Let me in!"

I'm too stunned to do anything but stand in front of the closed door, trembling. All this time, I've been thinking I'd never see him again, that he was not only gone but likely dead.

As if able to read my mind, the voice on the other side of the door, says, "Dammit, Sandy, don't you think if I were a ghost, I'd have slipped under the door already? Now, please, let me the hell in!"

I'm still not sure this isn't a dream, but then who else in their right mind would be out on a night like this, pounding on my door?

I fluff up my matted-down hair, wondering whether I should change out of my tattered "Menopausal Women for Pro-Choice" T-shirt. I haven't even brushed my teeth!

Another clap of thunder and all hesitation leaves me. I unlock the door. There's a flash of lightning, and there he is, backlit in the open doorway, just like the first time I saw him at the library all that time ago. That crooked grin, the turquoise eyes. Neptune has returned to Pilgrim's Landing!

"Jesus," I gasp, "you're not even wet!"

"It actually hasn't started raining yet. Just a preliminary noise-and-light show!"

I burst into tears and fall into his arms.

He's warm and has that familiar sea-salt smell.

"I really did think you were dead!" I say, my voice choking up. "I thought I had killed you!"

He holds me tight.

"It's okay, Sandy. It's okay." He rubs my back and runs his fingers through my hair.

I lean back so I can look at him. "Why didn't you write? Call? Anything!"

He turns, withdrawing his arms. "I brought you a present." He unzips a small duffle that's slung over one shoulder. He removes a beautiful pink-and-white shell with swirls on the top. "It's a conch shell." He holds it up to my ear. "If you're really quiet, you can hear the sound of the ocean."

I don't want to listen to a shell. I want answers.

"I don't know what to tell you," he says, "except that you don't really understand what it was like. All these people having this idea that I'd done something terrible—that was bad enough. But then, when you thought so, too?"

"I just wanted some answers. I didn't want you to leave." I open a drawer in the kitchen and find some matches to light the candle on the counter. I light the candle, and a small glowing nimbus springs up around us. Messi takes my hand and blows out the match.

"The truth was complicated," he says. "Is still complicated."

"Oh, bullshit, Messi."

I can't tell in the dim light if his eyes are serious or amused. "It took me time," he says. "To get past how I felt. Past my anger."

"When you just vanished in that storm, I had no idea where you were, or even if—"

"Key West. I sailed to Key West. I thought you would know."

"How would I know?"

"It was winter, and that's where I go to fish when it turns cold here."

I think of his stash of Cuban cigars. Fishing certainly isn't the only thing he goes there for.

"You should have let me know," I say.

"You're right. I should have." He laughs, pulls me back into his arms, and kisses me.

"Do you know you talk too much, Miss Librarian? That's no way to welcome home your sailor man who just returned from a rough passage."

He kisses me again, picks me up, and carries me into the bedroom, laying me down on the bed. I've gotten over my shock at seeing him again, alive and well, and once more in my—actually his—cottage on Frogs Neck Road. But beneath my happiness is a knot of rage. At him—but also at me. And yet—I can't stop my body from listing irresistibly in his direction. Where is my pride in all this? He just shows up, after disappearing without a trace, presumed dead for more than two months, and I'm supposed to jump right into bed with him as if he never left?

He lifts up my T-shirt. "You really could use some better night clothes," he says, admiring my naked breasts. "Correction. You look best with no night gear."

What is wrong with me?

With every bit of will I can muster, I pull back from him, covering my breasts with my hands, and say, "You can't just come here in the middle of the night after all this time and expect me to welcome you with open arms!"

He runs his fingers over my cheek and brushes back a strand of my hair. His face, usually so smooth, is wind-rough. He needs a shave. Has he really just anchored in a stormy sea? He smells like rain.

"I promise I'll tell you everything, Sandy. I promise. Just not tonight. Tonight, all I want to do is hold you in my arms, and drink you in, and not worry about the past or the future."

Despite myself, I give in, settle down beside him, wind my legs around his and welcome him back to Pilgrim's Landing.

And then—I suppose a fitting punishment for my weakness—when I awake in the morning, he's gone.

***

I say nothing to anyone at the library, including Ellen, but by the following day, it seems everyone knows Messi is back. He's been seen at Mohicans Bar, at a seafood fest at Sands End, and crossing Main Street in the rain.

It makes my blood boil, because he's made no attempt to see me again, and I'm still waiting for the promised conversation we desperately need to have where he'll "tell me everything."

In its way, this new disappearing act is even more infuriating than the months-long absence that preceded it. Who does Messi think he is, anyway? He's just a small-town fisherman, engaged in some shady business to make a few more bucks. Shady business? He might even be a murderer!

And yet... I can't stop thinking about him. And I can't make myself hate him. Damn him to hell! What's behind his seemingly irresistible pull, anyway?

His energy? How he embodies the rhythms of the sea—forever rolling in and receding? Or is it just that he's always surprising me, showing me sides of myself I didn't know existed before I met him?

The only thing I know is that when I'm with him, I feel alive. He calls me Wonder Woman sometimes because of the white streak in my hair, and when I'm with him, I *feel* like Wonder Woman, like I can do anything.

It's not fair, though. And I don't just mean for me. You see, when Messi disappeared, when I thought he was dead, I started seeing this man in town, Richard Forrest Wilson, hoping it would help me heal my aching heart. Dickie was a wealthy local landowner and real estate developer, one of those three-named natives of Pilgrims Landing who traced his heritage back to the *Mayflower*. I had no real interest in trading one rich dude, my ex-husband, for another rich dude, but when the wind howled outside my little cottage, there were nights when the loneliness was nearly unbearable, and Dickie offered comfort and a not unwelcome companionship.

Now, Messi's return has punched a hole in that little construct. No matter how fickle, unreliable and maddening he is, Messi's reappearance has made me realize I want him in my life, that I can't settle. The problem is to figure out how to do it without losing all self-respect.

When he calls me out of the blue after a week, saying, "How about some night fishing, tonight, darling? The moon is full," I almost have to laugh at his audacity.

"Sorry. I'm busy tonight," I say.

"What about tomorrow?"

"Not sure, probably busy."

Silence on the other end of the line. Messi isn't used to refusals.

"You're not the only man in town," I say to fill the silence.

"So I hear."

"You do realize that I thought you were dead?"

"Well, you certainly didn't mourn me very long."

"Why don't you give me a call tomorrow and I'll let you know if I'm free."

He laughs again, seemingly amused by the sudden difficulty he's having in pinning me down. But the next day comes and goes, and he never calls.

I can see this is not a game I'm going to win. At least not on my terms.

I have an old friend who always says to me that if she's able to land an interview, she knows she'll get the job. I feel a little that way about Messi. I'm certain if I can spend enough time with him, he'll lose interest in other women.

And so *I* call *him* the next day and tell him I hear the bluefish are running, especially at night. He doesn't follow through right away. It takes him another night, but then he does, and we head out in his boat again, just like we did before, and we swim and make love in the sea, and time stands still. Back on shore, at the cottage, we make love again, and afterwards, as we lie there, I remind him that we still haven't had the conversation he promised me.

I can feel him sigh, though I can't see it because my head is on his chest.

"What do you want to know?"

"Everything."

"That would take years. What you really want to know is if I killed Marna."

I nod.

"You can relax then. No one killed Marna. Marna's not dead."

I shoot straight up, disengaging, leaning back away from him, supported by an arm.

"She's alive?"

"You know, before she became an addict, we were together for four years. The drugs turned her into a different person. A person I couldn't stomach being around. She knew how I felt about it, and it made her not want to be around me. So she left. I didn't hear from her for over a year. Then the hospital in Sands End called one day. She was pregnant and had given them my number. The baby wasn't mine. The father of the child was Letitia Rose's son, Luke, a heroin addict like her, who died of an overdose while she was pregnant.

"Her parents had sold their house and moved. No one knew where. So, she literally was all alone. I stayed with her in the hospital till the baby was born. Then I brought them back here for a couple of days, and after that, to Key West. I had friends there who could look after them."

"You brought her to your house in Key West?"

"Not my house. I couldn't stand to see her. Or the boy. It wasn't his fault, but I couldn't stand looking at him. There'd been a time I thought Marna would have my child."

Messi gets up from the bed.

"And?"

"Well, that didn't happen, did it?"

"That was over two years ago, Messi. Are you trying to tell me that's not where you were all these months? I imagine she's clean now. I'm also guessing the rent money I pay you for the cabin on Frogs Neck Road you give to her. Meaning, in effect, I'm supporting her. She's who you went running off to in that crazy storm."

"It didn't happen that way. I didn't have a plan. I was just trying to survive. One of my engines conked out, the boat took on water. It was a hell of a thing. I was at sea for over two weeks."

"But eventually you made your way down to Key West. To her."

Messi sighs. "You're a hard woman, Sandy. Yes. I saw her when I finally got back to land. I was cold, hungry. I wanted..."

"Sex."

"No. Yes. I wanted comfort. I wanted warmth. I wanted a welcome from someone who would be happy to see me."

"So, it was me who sent you back to Marna's bed? "

"You sent me away—that's for sure."

What a bastard! "You could have told me all this before you made love to me."

Now it's Messi's turn to get mad. "And what good would that have done either one of us? I wanted you. You wanted me. Life happens. I care about you. And I care about Marna—but I'm here now and she's there."

"So, it's just out of sight, out of mind?"

He pulls me up and points out the window at the bay below.

"I'm not gonna be put in a box just to make you feel better. I'm sorry, but that's not who I am. I'm a sailor—my survival depends on happenstance, improvisation. I can't be held to someone else's program."

I'm not buying it. "Do you actually have a girl in every port? Are you that much of a cliché?"

"How can you ask me that? I didn't plan to see Marna again. I didn't plan to fall for you. It just happened."

"I left my husband after 20 years of marriage because he was unfaithful."

Messi shakes his head. "I don't believe that. If you did, you're a very foolish woman, and I don't believe you're a foolish woman. There must have been other reasons."

He's right, even though I don't want to give him that. It's true that I'd told my husband and our friends that I ended the marriage because of my husband's affair with the French bartender. But the real truth? I was tired of being married.

"I had no interest in making dinner for him and his banker colleagues anymore. I was tired of picking up after him, tired of doing his laundry."

Messi laughs. "Well, you already know that I'm more than happy to cook for both of us," he says. "And you've seen that I pick up after myself. I'm also pretty sure no one's ever accused me of being boring.... The way I see it, Sandy, you're way ahead of the game."

I have to laugh. Still. I can't view my relationship with him as a game. I want him all to myself. I want him to want me so much he'll give up everyone and everything else.

I guess I am a foolish woman, after all.

"I care about you, Sandy," he says, turning those impossibly blue eyes on me full force. "I hope you can accept the part of me that I can give you."

It's maddening. Am I supposed to accept the idea that some of Messi is better than none? It's so arrogant of him. I deserve better.

"I'm just supposed to wait for you to knock on my door in the middle of the night and let you in, no questions asked? What if I have other plans? Or someone else in my bed?"

"You mean Dickie? If he's my only competition, I'm not going to lose any sleep over it. But I won't only bang on your door in the middle of the night. I can find sex anywhere. I want much more from you. I want to take you fishing.

I want to show you the hot springs I've found. I want to cook for you and teach you to eat a clam. I want to read books with you...."

"How do I know you won't be thinking of Marna while you're making love to me?"

"If I call out her name in the middle of it, that'll be a clue!"

"You think this is funny?"

"Oh, Sandy. Let it go. Let it go. I can't predict what my relationship will be with Marna in the future—or with you. I don't even know if I'll have a future. What I do know—what I'm certain of—is that you and I can have a really good time together."

In the Seventies, they called the kind of arrangement he's advocating an open relationship. The Mormons were able to make this sort of thing work. There are even books about it. Issac Bashevis Singer's *Enemies, A Love Story,* about a man with two wives, and Jorge Amado's *Dona Flor and Her Two Husbands*, which I actually prefer. I ask Messi if he's ever read the latter, though I already know the answer.

"What's it about?" he asks.

"A woman whose first husband is very sexy but also unfaithful and barely scraping by financially. After he dies, she marries a pharmacist, who's a great provider, but a very boring lover. They make love once a week at the same time. When the dead husband returns as a ghost, he makes fun of the new husband's lovemaking skills. The point, I suppose, is that one person can never satisfy all our needs."

"Well—if it's in a book," Messi says, "then we know it must be telling the truth about the human heart."

He leads me to the door of the cottage, and then walks me up to the road to where I've stashed my bike.

"Will I see you again?" he asks.

"Does the moon control the tides?" I tease.

I remember what he said the night I threw him out in the storm, after I accused him of not caring about me. His reply still echoes in my ears. "You mean a great deal to me, but you are not everything."

Will that always be true? I know he's right, that we can have some fun. But will that ever be enough?

A thought enters my mind like a black cloud passing in front of the sun.

Would I be happier if Messi confessed that he murdered Marni instead of becoming her lover?

The question lingers unanswered, like an itch I can't scratch. I can't help but wonder what other mischief Neptune and Diana might casually toss my way...

Will I ever get any answers? Do I even want them?

Or is it my fate to be alone?

I guess only time will tell.

Made in the USA
Middletown, DE
13 September 2023

38160273R00120